Artifice Layer

By David Robert Retro

Visit <u>Amazon</u> for more books by David Robert Retro.

© 2024 David Robert Retro.
All rights reserved.

This book is dedicated to nostalgia, I am haunted by you.

Chapter One
A Bump in The Road.

The bump in the road, although minor, was enough to remove the steering wheel from the chauffeur's hands. Momentarily of course, he's a professional.

'What was that?' I call out from the back of the limo. It's a long distance between me and him, I've never ridden in a limo before, I'm not keen. He doesn't answer, maybe he didn't hear me. It's dark already but he took my watch and phone from me when we met, so I have no idea what time it is. The party was supposed to start at half past four. I may have to be fashionably late.

In amongst these last few miles, with a late December sundown supporting a lonely wilderness on either side, I spy a grandiose country manor, set back from the road. The first and only sign of other life. It must be the place.

The car slows down at a gated entrance on the left. The chauffeur slides his window down and stares at an entrance box that is directly aligned with his face. After a moment, the gates begin to part, the chauffeur slides his window up and gently eases forward. We begin along an elaborate, elevated and winding entrance path with various, festive ornaments adorning random foliage on either side.

Eventually we turn into a large courtyard, with the classic circular arrival and middle court fountain. The car stops at the foot of the entrance stairs, the chauffeur exits the vehicle and, in a flash, has my door open. I emerge apologetically and stare up towards the great oak double doors.

'So, this is where Doc lives?' I say, with a child-like wonder.

The chauffeur smiles at me in the affirmative. Well, I say smile, it's also kind of a grimace. Either way, he's quickly back in the car and driving off, out of sight. I guess that's that.

I tackle the stairs and knock the knocker on the door. A tall and well-built man-mountain opens it, almost immediately.

'Invitation?' he says.

I search in my pocket and pass him the evidence. He studies it carefully and, seeming satisfied, relaxes his demeanour.

'Follow it to the right, Sir.' he says.

I nod and do indeed, "follow it to the right."

The hallway, with hanging blankets forming a path and blocking any sight of the main part of the entrance hall, leads to an open door, wherein lies what appears to be a makeshift medical unit. There's a gurney next to a machine that registers vitals, and one of them stand-up trolleys that carry blood bags and transparent liquids. It's all a bit clinical. I stand there, alone, wondering what's going on. To add to the confusion, the door which I used to enter the room is shut behind me and I hear it locked from the other side. I look around the room again but there's not much in here to offer any answers.

Suddenly, at the other end of the cubicle, the walls part and a familiar face enters. It's Doc, the man who I met when paying my contribution to the organisation. The scientist, the leader, the owner of this beautiful country manor and most importantly, the party thrower.

'Clifford!' he says warmly, 'You're late!' 'I know, I'm sorry, traffic..'

'Traffic? It's the middle of nowhere man!'

He smiles and embraces me, though we don't know each other terribly well so it's a bit awkward.

'Follow me old boy, our guests are waiting, I hope you're okay with lifts?' he says, darting back from whence he came and scuttling across the grand entrance hall, now in full sight. I half run, just to keep pace.

'What?'

'Lifts, dear boy, elevators. Some people get claustrophobic.' 'Oh, no, I'm fine.' I say.

'Jolly good.' he says, stopping in front of it and pressing the button. The doors open and we both climb aboard.

'Lower Floor.' he says loudly. The doors close and we begin our descent.

'I can't believe you have a lift in your house, how many floors are there?' I say. 'Twelve.' he replies.

'And you speak to it, there's no buttons?'

'There are buttons, but I prefer voice command these days.'

The elevator slows to a stop and the doors slide open, revealing a dingy corridor. Doc looks at me and raises his eyebrow.

'The Bowels!' he exclaims before pacing off. 'Come!'

I jog after him, following the corridor left and right, like a typical funhouse, complete with uneven floors. Disorientated, the corridor finally opens into a room that looks like a small cinema. Five lines of maybe twenty chairs, facing a stage, or a plinth really, the flooring is of a similar height to the rest of the room. Most of the chairs have people in them. They're all looking at me. I smile at them, with a hint of embarrassment and self-loathing. Doc is on the stage, standing in front of a large curtain that flows the length of it.

'Come on Clifford, take a seat old boy, let's get started.'

I sit on an end chair in front of me. The next seat is vacant and a woman sits in the next, though she doesn't watch me, she's watching Doc.

'Welcome everyone and thank you for attending.' he says, addressing the room. 'As we're running late, I'll get through this quickly, time is nobody's friend!' He pauses for any sign of recognition but no-one reacts.

'Right then, you have been invited here this evening, on behalf of the Krelboyne Institute, as our most valued investors of our scientific research. The money that you have provided has allowed us to advance technologies in our endeavours to produce the very best artificial intelligence.

The work that we have achieved over the last eighteen months in particular, has been nothing short of remarkable and we have decided to share it with the people who have enabled that. You.'

Doc pauses and stands proudly in front of his audience. I see fellow patrons glance excitedly at each other. He continues.

'Behind this curtain is the fruits of our labour, the leading technology in its field. You, my friends, are the first to see it. Behold!'

Doc moves to the side of the stage, backwards, holding his

gaze to the centre of the curtain, arms outstretched. It's very dramatic. One of his arms reaches for a draping rope at the side and he yanks it. The curtain that stretches the length of the stage drops to the floor, revealing its secrets. Bewilderment swirls the room.

Running the length of the stage, angled slightly downwards, a large mirror reflects back at the audience. I can see that everyone is sharing the look of confusion.

'I'm sure you're all wondering what you're looking at? Let me explain.' Doc walks back to the centre of the stage, enjoying the mystery.

'May I introduce our Operations Director, Alex Forrester.'

Again, he holds his arms outstretched towards a stage door to the right, full of pomp and circumstance, poise and concentration, very formal. He looks mental.

From the door, a small, wiry woman, casually dressed, shuffles onto the stage. Eyes down, the polar opposite of Doc and his powerful theatrics. She seems awkward and talks with no emotion and a brisk delivery.

'We have created a robot that emulates human behaviour and characteristics, combining cutting-edge technology with a deep understanding of human cognition. With vast amounts of data and training models, and advanced algorithms, we were able to develop a neural network capable of comprehending language, context and emotions. This neural network forms the core of the robot's cognitive abilities, enabling it to engage in natural and fluid conversations, understand nuanced meanings, and even empathise with the human condition. To replicate human-like physicality, we employed advanced materials and engineering techniques to construct a sophisticated robotic framework, complete with intricate sensors and actuators, enabling the robot to mimic human movements with astonishing accuracy. Additionally, we incorporated computer vision systems, allowing the robot to perceive its surroundings and interact with objects in a manner that closely resembles human perception. The integration of these technological components, combined with tireless iterations and refinements, culminated in the successful creation of a robot that blurs the line between man and machine.'

Alex offers an awkward smile and quickly leaves the stage. The mirror shows everyone

open-mouthed, questioning everything, and unsure whether to clap. Doc addresses us again. 'Alex will remain here in the property for any questions or testing. As of now, you are cordially invited to a whodunnit with a twist! There are thirteen of you in this room, twelve of you are our most valued investors, one of you is our creation.' He pauses for effect. 'But who?'

I, along with everyone else seated, look suspiciously around. They all seem real. No obvious skinjobs. A man in the front row stands.

'Why don't you just tell us?' he says.

'Where would the fun be in that, Thomas? And besides, if you guess correctly there's a prize.' Thomas slowly sits back down.

'I'm listening.'

Doc looks at his watch.

'It's 17:28, we will go through the atrium to the biodome for champagne and get to know one another. The bell will toll at 18:00 hours and each of you will choose who you believe is the robot. The votes will be counted and whoever has the most votes will be blood tested in front of the rest of you to determine if they are in fact synthetic or not. If correct, the people who voted correctly will each receive a prize. If the vote is incorrect, the person who received the most votes will be ejected from the gathering and the game will continue. Every so often, we will vote again until the robot is revealed. There will be food, drink and other entertainment available throughout the duration. Personally, I think we may need it, as I believe in the science and am anticipating a late night. However, you're obviously all shrewd investors and should you discover the creation immediately, the offer of our hosting your evening remains. Before we move this soiree, are there any other questions?'

The woman next to me speaks. 'What's the prize?'

Doc smiles.

'You tell me!' he says, with the usual mystery. 'Come!'

He jets off the stage and disappears back down the corridor we entered through. Slowly, everyone, me included, chase after him. I take the opportunity to study the other guests more closely. I can't see any visible signs that would give the game away.

'It's cosy!' Doc says, as everyone packs into the lift.

As we make our ascent, I realise that everyone is eyeing everyone else, looking for any subtle sign, to no avail. If there is a robot in here, they've done a marvellous job.

'One rule,' Doc says quietly, 'no cutting, no blood, if this rule is broken, no prize.'

The elevator stops, spewing us back into the main hall. We follow Doc through a maze of corridors, into an atrium with an impressive skylight. The sun is setting, and a misty rain is beginning to take hold.

It's a large room and at the end of the walkway, where most people would have a conservatory, we enter an even larger biodome. Lined with bizarre plantations and shrubs and crops, tall and overarching the pathways like a huge forest or jungle. A table with glasses of bubbly is front and centre.

'Please, help yourselves, get to know one another, peruse the woodland, I shall return!'

With that, Doc turns tail and vanishes, leaving a group of strangers, standing in a forest, with alcohol. A few guests have already chosen their weapon, so I decide to do the same.

'Well, I'm Amelia.' one woman says, taking a large gulp from her glass. 'Viola.' says another.

'Hang on, hang on, I'm never gonna remember all these names. Let's try this the easy way. Who here is a robot?'

The man who spoke, slugs his drink down in one. No one speaks.

'Okay, not surprising but you never know. So, I'll take the lead here, I don't wanna be playing games all evening. My name's Thomas or Tommy and here's my idea. We pair up, show each other our tonsils. I doubt they've been as particular with the internal workings. We should find our culprit, quick enough.'

People are already walking toward each other and exposing their throats. Examinations are being considered. The woman who addressed herself as Amelia walks towards me, mouth agape. I get a good view of things and consider it normal. I give a nod of approval.

'Now you.' she says.

I return the manoeuvre. She gets way too close, swaying around like a dentist. Eventually, she leans back, satisfied. I feel okay closing my jaw. We look around, everyone else seems satisfied with what they've seen. Thomas scratches his chin, deep in thought. Nobody has found anything suspicious to say.

'Let's be pragmatic. It's a robot…'

He stares at us, one by one. An older woman begins to speak but Thomas makes a sharp noise and gestures for silence. She looks offended and rightly, it was quite rude. Our self-elected leader is enjoying the authoritative role, we wait for his next assertion.

'It's in the eyes. I'm counting four of us who have glasses on. They're not gonna make a robot with bad eyesight. Who's got contact lenses? Let's see hands.'

I wear glasses, it makes sense. Two women raise their hands. 'So that makes six, what about corrective surgery?'

The seven remaining people put their hands up. 'You've all had laser eye surgery?'

They look apologetic while Thomas mutters and shakes his head in disbelief.

'Well then, we've got ourselves a liar.' he says, walking up to me and taking his glasses off. 'Let's see 'em.'

We swap glasses and wear each other's, testing our need for wearing them.

'And you two.' Thomas indicates to the other two four-eyed ladies. They follow suit. He gives me my glasses back and the deed is done. The four of us seem convinced by the bad eyesight. 'The two with the contacts, take 'em out.' he says.

The lady who he offended earlier is one of them. 'Who put you in charge?' she says curtly.

Thomas grimaces.

'What's your name sweetheart?'

She clearly doesn't like that and he knows it. 'Claire.'

'Well look Claire, I came here to relax and have a nice time, not to play games all evening. I suspect you want the same, so I'm trying to solve this as quick as possible, darling.'

'Don't call me darling, or are you naturally patronising?'

'Alright, alright, don't get your knickers in a twist. I just think a man can think more clearly in a difficult situation. Call me old-fashioned. I'm just trying to get us all through this, efficiently.' Claire shakes her head. Thomas has clearly offended her and everyone else for that matter. 'I was gonna offer you a shovel to dig that hole but you seem to be doing just fine.' she says. Thomas smiles sarcastically. A younger, handsome man interjects.

'Why don't we pair up and wander around the biodome, get a feel for the other person, we'll meet back here and discuss.'

A woman joins in.

'It's a good idea. There doesn't seem to be any obvious physical tells. Perhaps something in their personality will give them away,' she says, 'I'm Alex by the way, another Alex.'

The younger man links arms with her and has one of the other women linked on the other arm. 'There's an odd number so we'll do the threesome.' he says confidently.

Alex doesn't seem to mind and the other woman is giggling. They collect another drink each and head off down a path, laughing bawdily.

'I guess we're doing that then.' says Viola, gesturing for another woman to join her.

They saunter off down another path together, introducing themselves. Looking around, others are pairing up and wandering off. Thomas contemptuously offers his arm to Claire, who sneers and walks off with another man. A tall, older man stands by the drinks table, quaffing and relaxed. Thomas is looking at me, I'm trying not to meet his gaze, guilt by association. The only other person left is Amelia, who thankfully grabs my arm and leads me away. We make our way along a thin, winding walkway, admiring the lavish undergrowth.

'What's your name?'

'Cliff,' I say, 'and you're Amelia.' 'Correct. How come you were late?'

'Uh, there was roadworks on the outskirts of my village.' 'Okay, who do you think the robot is?'

I smile. She's sweating me.

'Uh, I dunno. The guy back there with Thomas looks suspicious. He's just hanging out next to the alcohol.'

'I talked to him earlier, his name's Avon, I think he's South African. We were the first people here.'

It's my turn with the questions. 'Who was first to arrive?'

'Me.' she says.

'Who do you think the robot is?' I ask.

'Well, I don't know who the robot is but I know who I'm voting for. That misogynistic piece of shit.'

'Thomas?' I offer.

'Yeah, what a douche. I don't fancy spending time in his company all evening. What did you think, or do you share a similar view?' she says, smiling mischievously.

'Yeah, it was pretty rude, if he thinks that way, he should probably keep his opinions to himself.' 'Especially amongst strangers!' she says.

'Yeah.'

'Anyway, I doubt they'd make a robot with such outdated views, spouting rubbish and nonsense. I'm still gonna vote for him though, what a prick.'

Amelia finishes her drink and freezes, admiring a massive bean arch in a small clearing. At one end is a dog bed and a bowl of water. No dog though. We share a glance.

'I guess there's a dog around here!' she says excitedly.

'Yeah,' I say, 'dogs are pretty intuitive, maybe it can smell us and be able to tell the difference between human and…not human.'

'Have you got any pets?' she says. 'Yeah, two cats, you?'

'Yeah, I've got a dog, a basset hound, Nathan.' 'Nathan? I've never known a dog called Nathan?' 'Well now you do.' says Amelia.

Early days but we're getting on rather well, I hope she isn't a robot. I think we share natural conversation, it's easy. Her attention is drawn behind us. Two women have entered the same area. I haven't met either of them but Amelia seems to know them both.

'Hello again,' Amelia says, 'this is Cliff.' I offer them both a semi wave.

'I'm Elizabeth, this is Kay. We've been admiring the exotic greenery around here, remarkable! And they have Palm trees with coconuts growing!' she says.

'They must use different temperatures in different areas to maintain the various cultivation necessary!' Kay remarks.

'Yes, it's certainly impressive.' I say. It is. 'What have you seen?' she asks.

'Uhhh, that bean arch.' I say, unimpressively. Amelia saves me. 'There's a dog bed over there, have either of you seen a dog?'

'No, gladly, I'm not keen on dogs. They can be very…strong-willed.' Elizabeth says, looking nervously around.

'So, is he a robot?' Kay asks Amelia, obviously referring to me. 'I don't think so, not with that haircut.' she says, hopefully joking. 'Well, we ran into Claire and… what was his name?'

'Teddy' says Elizabeth. Kay continues.

'We ran into Claire and Teddy and she's going to vote for Thomas. I think Teddy will too. He wasn't happy with what he said and Claire was very cross. She asked us to vote for him. We said we would. I mean it was so rude wasn't it? How awful.'

Kay and Elizabeth are genuine. Amelia responds.

'We're gonna vote for him too, we've only been here for five minutes and he's crossing the line already.'

'I know,' Kay says, 'well, if you see her, she's bound to ask. Have you seen anyone else?' 'No, you?'

'We saw that younger chap and the two ladies.' Kay says. Elizabeth chimes in.

'They'd found a private beach type area and they were frolicking about. I should think he's more interested in finding a mate as opposed to a robot.' she says, clearly offended by the behaviour. 'They were only enjoying themselves.' Kay tries.

'Mmmmm.'

The noise hangs in the air.

'Well, see you later then,' Amelia says, 'keep an eye out for the dog!' We part ways and continue our jaunt around the gardens.

'We should look for that beach!'

'Beach type area,' I say, 'there's not gonna be an actual beach in here.' 'We'll see.'

We turn a corner and the plants and general environment becomes more exotic looking. A table in front of us is peppered with cocktails, champagne and obligatory ice buckets.

'Can you smell the sea air?' she says, grinning at me.

We help ourselves to a cocktail and wander in between overhanging palm trees, the path turning into sand beneath our feet. It opens into a huge, enclosed beach. On one side of the area, a large swimming pool with diving boards assist an impressive, tropical vista. Sitting on the beach, chatting and laughing, are the group of three. The young man is topless, revealing an impressive physique and enjoying the fake temperatures on this side of the biodome. He notices us and beckons us over. We do it.

'Hey guys, I'm Desmond, this is Alex and Agatha.' he says, introducing his fanclub. 'This is Cliff, I'm Amelia, I see you've found the best seats in the house?' she grins.

'Amazing isn't it?' he says. 'So warm, table full of drinks, we're stopping here man, even the water in the pool is heated!'

'He didn't think there'd be a beach in here,' Amelia says, nodding at me, 'what do you think now Cliff, are you feeling overdressed?'

'What can I say, I'm definitely feeling overdressed.' I laugh.

We all enjoy the scenery for a moment, it's difficult to describe when you consider the different areas in the same building. It's a fake paradise.

'Have you seen a dog?' Amelia asks. The three look confused. Agatha speaks. 'No. Is there a dog?'

'Well, we saw a bowl and a bed so there is evidence of a dog but nothing solid.' says Amelia. 'Have you guys talked about the robot?' Alex says.

'We have a bit. I think everyone is voting for Thomas though.' 'After what he said to Claire?' asks Desmond.

'Yeah, I think people were put out by it.' 'It was rude.' he says.

'What about you guys?' Amelia continues, 'Any ideas?'

Agatha and Desmond smile, glancing at each other. Alex speaks.

'Well, we talked and came to the conclusion that it's too early to tell, obviously. We haven't spent time with everyone yet so until then, we were gonna hang out here as much as possible, because it's awesome. We were gonna vote for him, (pointing at me) but now you've mentioned Thomas, we'll maybe vote for him instead?' she says, asking the other two.

They both nod in agreement. I'm taken aback.

'Why were you gonna vote for me?' I say, as calmly as I can muster.

'You were the last one here. It was kinda suspicious. Plus, you've got that look about you.' Amelia laughs. They all laugh. Even I laugh.

'Anyway, we're gonna vote for Thomas now so relax, you're safe this time.' 'Until next time…' says Desmond. Cheeky sod.

Into the clearing, another two women enter. One is Viola, who introduced herself earlier. I don't know the other woman, who is talking excitedly about the beach area. She runs towards the swimming pool. Viola approaches our group, looking spent.

'Are you alright?' Amelia asks.

'Yeah, yeah, it's her, she goes on and on, it's a bit tiring.'

'What's her name?'

'Clemence, or Clem. She owns property around the world and likes talking about it. Comparing everything we see with a property she owns here or there; it's exhausting.'

Desmond smiles. 'Thomas has got competition then.' 'No, no, she's harmless I think, just…hard work.' 'You don't think she's the robot?'

'I don't know. We saw Claire earlier and she asked us both to vote for Thomas this time, you know, because he was quite obnoxious.'

'What did you say?'

'We said we would, neither of us want to spend the evening listening to him. We saw him with Avon when we went back for a drink and he was being quite opinionated, poor Avon looked a bit sad,' she says, 'have you noticed the cameras set up around here?'

We all shake our heads.

'They've got cameras set up, here and there. They're probably watching us.' 'Who's they?' Desmond says.

'I don't know, Doc and that dull woman on the stage earlier?'

'Why?'

'I don't know. We'll ask.'

Clem wanders over, smiling like a maniac.

'This is a wonderful spot! It reminds me of a property I own in Italy! My one has real sea water going into the pool area but still, it's lovely! Have you guys settled here for now? I bet you have, it's wonderful!'

'Viola rolls her eyes, making sure we can all see her reaction. The rest of us attempt straight faces. Clem cracks on.

'I've got another place in Jamaica, well, two actually, that have the palm trees like the ones here. It's amazing how they grow all the tropical things, very clever!'

She takes a handful of sand and examines it closely, before letting it slip through her fingers. 'You know, I own a property in Bahrain, quite an exclusive area, near where they do the formula one racing, me and my husband normally go. This sand is almost identical. Same colour, same feel, it's uncanny.'

'Really?' says Viola, playing along. Clem doesn't pick up on the sarcasm. 'Yeah. Amazing!'

'Well, we'll keep on exploring. Come on robot, I mean Cliff!' Amelia says. I smile. 'O-K.' I say, in my best robot voice.

We say goodbye and stroll off the beach, back to the path. 'Clem seems like hard work.'

'Yeah, no wonder Viola is frustrated.' I say.

The landscape begins to evolve into a woodland, heavily armed trees and bushes lean into us and fill the distance on either side. It's a darker area.

'Come on,' she says, 'let's go off-road.'

She cuts off of the path and ventures into the thick undergrowth. I follow, easing branches away and stumbling carefully through fallen leaves. It's very realistic, considering it's all "inside".

Amelia reaches the dome glass and sits on a low tree branch. She takes a cigarette from her pocket and offers me one. I accept and we both light.

'Thanks.' I say.

'No worries, the driver took all my shit. Phone, keys but I was allowed to bring smokes, you?' 'Yeah, the driver took everything, part of the game, I didn't bring smokes, stupidly.'

'You think the robot smokes?' she asks.

'I don't know. Everyone looks real to me, maybe.'

'Do you think the robot knows it's a robot? I've seen loads of shows where the robot doesn't know. If it doesn't know, it could be you or me. If I've been implanted with a past and memories and traits…I'm just not gonna know.'

'I know.'

We both smoke, contemplating the situation. On the other side of the glass, it's raining hard. It's dark and it seems like there's a large field out there but it's difficult to tell. The rainfall is peppering the glass though.

'The thing is, there must be a tell. I assumed it would be a physical tell, the eyes or the gait, something off, you know, not quite right.'

Amelia nods. 'There isn't though, nothing obvious anyway.'

'There doesn't seem to be, no. Maybe after this exercise, someone will have noticed something apparent with their partner and that will be that. But in the lift, I was looking at everyone up close and I'm telling you…it's good.'

She crosses her legs and leans back onto a well-placed nook.

'I was the first one here so I got a good look at everyone when they arrived. Apart from you,' she says, half-jokingly, 'I didn't spot anything.'

'So, if it isn't a physical tell, it has to be an internal tell, a gap in the database.'

'I'm not sure, it's got to be easier to act like a human as opposed to looking like one.' I concede. She's right.

'So what do we do?'

'I think we should stick to the physical for now. Maybe we'll play parlour games and discover someone who can't throw darts!' Until then, we'll all vote for Thomas and that self-absorbed woman on the beach.'

We both laugh. 'Okay.'

Amelia sits silently, smoking and staring into the ether. I think about my family, my past and the idea that I could be a robot. All of these memories that aren't really mine. Would a robot be so philosophical? Probably. How would you know? How could you? If you sit at the poker table for thirty minutes and can't spot the mug, it's probably you.

I watch Amelia, studying her hands, her lips as she smokes, her hair follicles, her ear cavities. It's all real. As real as real can be. She turns towards me. I think she noticed my leering. I quickly look away and finish my smoke.

'Cliff.'

I turn to her.

'Look at me.' she says.

We sit looking at each other's faces, only thirty centimetres apart. Carefully checking each feature and considering the curvatures of the forehead and cheekbone, for what feels like an eternity. It's intimate.

'Anything?' she says, finally. 'No, you.'

'No.'

We both relax back, the intensity wanes from our postures. Amelia lets out a huge sigh. Not unhappy, more perplexed.

'Let me look at your hands.' she says, reaching out.

I give her my left hand. She takes it and begins studying, turning it this way and that.

'You're older than you look. Hands are a giveaway. People

cover their faces with all that cream but if you look at someone's hands, they're very revealing. You can tell a lot about a person based on their hands.'

She's right, I am older than I look.

Can you tell if they belong to a robot though?' I say.

'I would say that these hands don't. What about mine?'

She thrusts her right hand towards me, I take it and begin to investigate the movements of the fingers, the lines and the blemishes on the palm, the nails, the thumb, the smooth texture around the knuckles.

'No,' I say, 'I think they're real.'

I release her hand back to her.

'Have you noticed any cameras?' she says.

'I haven't,' I reply, gazing around, 'I haven't been looking to be honest.'

'Well, I have been looking, no joy though, it's too dark in here, let's head back to the path and see what we see.'

Amelia stands, stretches and begins to make her way back. I follow cautiously. As we reach the track, a loud clock chimes, the sound encompassing the entire dome. We freeze, staring at each other as six chimes bellow out. The forest falls silent.

'That must be the time?'

'It seemed to go quickly. They made sure we weren't wearing watches so I guess we'll have to trust that that is the time.' she says.

'So what happens now?'

'I guess we head back to the entrance and see if there's any drinks left.' Amelia winks and starts walking in the opposite direction from where we entered this point.

'Shouldn't we go back the way we came?' I try.

'It probably circles round.' she shouts, disappearing around a corner.

I hotstep after her, the gloom of the woods is left behind and replaced with an English country garden vibe. Extravagant horticulture lines the path and the temperature has warmed up again. 'Looks like we're late.' she says, gesturing up ahead.

I see the entrance where we came into the biodome. Doc is there, deep in conversation with several guests. The drinks table looks seriously depleted but not defunct, thankfully. I could use another.

As we approach, voices hush, and everyone turns to us.

'Here they are, that's ten. We're just waiting for the group of three,' Doc says, 'have you seen them?'

'They were on the beach. Is it six already?' Amelia says. 'Why not!' he says, with an unjustified amount of gusto.

I glance at the other guests to gauge their moods, wondering if any of them have discovered the perpetrator. It would appear not. They all seem like...well...like humans.

We hear giggling and cackling as Loverboy and the fanclub saunter up the path, arm in arm. Desmond is still topless, making sure everyone can enjoy his torso, they each help themselves to a drink and quieten down. Doc waits like a schoolteacher, for complete silence. His index finger, pressed to his lips, all eyes are on him.

'Come!' he shrieks, racing back through the atrium and into the entrance hall. We all chase after him, trying not to spill our drinks or fall over. It feels very "Crystal Maze" without the tracksuits.

The sheets that were obscuring our view when we arrived

earlier have been removed, revealing the entrance in its entirety. It's bigger than anywhere I've ever lived. A decorator's nightmare.

We follow Doc across the hall and into the sliding door which holds the strange medical unit. Alex Forrester is there, standing awkwardly next to the gurney. Everybody gathers around Doc and waits for the next instruction. He loves to build up the drama and we're all seeming to play along. The room, once again, falls silent.

'So here we are, thirteen become twelve. This is an open vote. I will go around the room, one by one, you will give me the name.' He pauses and widens his eyes. 'The first decision.'

Pensively, Amelia speaks.

'What happens if we don't vote?'

'Why on earth wouldn't you? Where's the fun in that?' Doc asks. 'I don't know, I'm just asking.' she says.

'Well I can't imagine why you wouldn't vote, you wouldn't win a prize.' 'What is the prize?'

'I told you earlier.' he says, struggling to keep his poise.

'You said "You tell me" earlier. What does that mean?' she probes. Doc sighs.

'If you guess correctly, you tell me what you would like as your prize.' 'What, anything?'

'Anything. Short of eternal life, everything is on the table.' he says.

At that moment, a man enters the room, through the sliding door and closes it firmly behind him. It bangs shut, drawing everyone's attention. It's the man who greeted me at the entrance. I use the term *greeted* loosely. He is a behemoth, nearly seven feet tall and as wide as a train. He doesn't look particularly friendly either. I would hate to meet him in a dark alley. In fact, I wouldn't fancy meeting him in a well-lit alley. He stands in front of the door, folds his arms and waits patiently. Doc smiles.

'Ah, everybody, meet Hendon. Hendon is our security on site, he's friendlier than he looks and is our local gardening expert. Do not play chess with him, he will destroy you. Do not damage anything in the gardens, he will destroy you. And, I suppose, needless to say, do not

arm-wrestle with him, he will destroy you.'

Hendon doesn't react to anything Doc says. His arrival brings an air of menace to the proceedings. Doc takes a clipboard from Alex F and stands before us.

'Let us begin.'

Chapter Two
The First Decision.

'The first decision!' Doc says, again. 'Thomas, say the name of the person who you think is not a person, please.'

Thomas can't stop a grin appearing on his face. 'Claire.'

Doc scribbles on his clipboard. 'Avon, vote please.'

Avon looks carefully around at everyone, I'm not sure what he'll do, he's been spending time with Thomas, the bookies favourite.

'What's his name?' he says, pointing at me. 'That's Cliff.' Doc says.

'Cliff.' Avon says. Doc scribbles my name on his clipboard.

Me? Bloody hell. Thanks Avon. I can't help but feel slightly offended. We've hardly met and he has me down as a skinjob? I was not expecting that. Doc isn't waiting for my emotional slide down the rabbit hole, he's called Teddy for a vote. We haven't talked either so maybe he'll vote for me as well. My internal paranoia is absolutely loving this.

'Thomas.' says Teddy.

Claire goes next and votes the same, as do Kay, Elizabeth,

Viola and Clem. Thomas is containing his rage and pretending it doesn't bother him. I'm calming down and enjoying someone else getting all of the attention, or all of the votes to be more accurate. 'Amelia, vote please.' Doc says.

She looks at me, taking pleasure from sweating me long enough to get my mind racing. 'Thomas.' she says.

Doc scribbles on his clipboard.

'The round is over. We have a result. Thomas has received seven votes and is therefore deemed to be the robot. All that remains is a simple blood test with instantaneous results to determine his makeup, synthetic or otherwise.'

I didn't have to vote, I feel strangely relieved that I didn't have to cast my opinion into the ring, I don't know why.

Thomas shakes his head; scorn riddles his face. He begins to roll his sleeve up.

'You were all offended by the way I spoke earlier. You weren't trying to find the robot. You're all too precious.'

'The way you were talking was out of order, it was chauvinistic, there's no room in society for thinking like that.' Claire says.

Thomas continues to shake his head.

'Why don't we all adjust to this new found, bullshit attitude, you can't speak your mind anymore. Whatever you say offends someone. Where do you want me?' he asks Doc.

'Next to the gurney please.'

Thomas walks over to the gurney and stands prostrate, eyeballing everyone else, trying to evoke a sense of guilt around the room. Alex F readies a needle and prods it into his arm. She takes what looks like blood, retracts the needle and crosses back to the desk. She then forces two drops onto a small, glass slide and injects it into a machine. A tiny screen in front of her lights up with an array of numbers, letters and symbols. It's a very dated looking piece of equipment, considering the modern environment that otherwise surrounds us.

After several seconds of scrolling, the screen goes blank and then projects three lines of statistics. A printout of said stats is ejected from the machine, similar to a receipt.

Doc takes it, turns and addresses us.

'Thomas is human. You are incorrect. The game continues. Thomas, you will be escorted back to your driver and your belongings by Hendon. Is there anything you'd like to say to the group?' Thomas has one last look around.

'No.' he says.

Hendon strides across the room with a blank expression and coaxes Thomas to the exit door. He walks expressionless and exits without looking back. Hendon follows.

'One moment please.' Doc says to the rest of us, while turning back to Alex F.

They enter into a deep discussion, pointing at things on the clipboard, Doc is quite animated, Alex, not so much. We can't make out what they're saying but watch their heads shaking and body movements closely. It's like a silent movie. Finally, it would appear that they have reached an agreement, Doc turns back to the group, clipboard in hand.

'Okay then, we continue. If I call your name, please follow Alex to the first-floor master study where she will give you instructions. Amelia, Agatha, Elizabeth, Teddy, Desmond and Clemence.'

Alex leads them through the sliding door and away. The rest of us wait. 'Okay, we should have Alex, Avon, Cliff, Kay, Claire and Viola.'

Doc glances at us as he calls our names, like calling a register before heading off to assembly. 'Right, we're off to the ground floor study, where I will give you your next instructions, come!' Again, he races off through the sliding door, we scurry after him like rats in a maze.

Across the entrance hall and along a richly furnished corridor, pictures and other objects of beauty adorn the walls and mantles. There's money everywhere. He stops in front of one of the many wooden doors along here, turns the key and beckons us in.

I am the first to arrive and I marvel at the huge, two-storey study. Filled with taxidermy mounts of a variety of animals, a large collection of books in bookshelves, which cover the upper section above us, a wonderful, stained-glass circular ceiling and a very welcome tray of drinks on one of the large oak desks in front of us.

Doc walks us to one side of the room, with luxurious sofas around a roaring fireplace. We circle around him, no one brave enough to plop down on the comfy chesterfields.

'First of all, the desk with the drinks on over there,' he points, 'has a box with a red button on it. If you press the button, I will be alerted and will come to you forthwith.'

We all look politely at the said button.

'Now, this time it will work like a jury, there are twelve of you, after all. You will discuss the other six guests and choose two of them as your most likely guesses for the automaton. When you have chosen, press the red button and I will come for your decision and explain the next steps. Please be aware that the other guests are selecting two of you for the same reason, so time is of the essence. Please help yourselves to drinks but do so responsibly. Any questions?'

'When will dinner be?' Alex asks. 'Dinner will be served in an hour or two.' 'Where's the toilet?' Avon asks.

'Most rooms have an en-suite, this one has one there.' Doc points at a stylish door across the room.

'Okay then, I'll see you soon.' he says, quickly exiting the room.

Avon walks to the toilet, the rest of us wander to the drinks table and get involved. There're all sorts to choose from, some look like soft drinks or cocktails. Nearly full bottles of whisky or rum stand in front of glasses made with a selection of mixers accompanying them. There's also pints of lager and ale, all of them ice cold.

The women help themselves to extravagant looking cocktails, Claire adds a liberal sprinkling of olives to hers. I take a pint of lager and swig. Yes, it's lager.

'Shall we sit on the sofas and discuss it?' Says Alex.

Everyone silently agrees and heads to the sofas. We sit down collectively and taste our drinks. 'Wow.' Claire says, clearly enjoying the flavour.

'It isn't useful now but I wonder how Avon got on with Thomas? He didn't vote for him, did he?' says Kay.

'He voted for you.' Viola says to me. 'I know,' I say, 'bit harsh.'

Avon exits the toilet, takes a pint of ale(maybe), and takes a seat next to me. 'Cheers.' he says, raising his glass to the group, before taking a generous slug. 'How was Thomas?' Viola says.

Everyone else is interested. Avon smiles shyly, he seems reserved.

'Like you'd imagine really. Quite brash and outspoken. I didn't say much but he didn't seem to mind holding court.'

'How come you voted for Cliff and not him?'

'Cliff turned up late so I was a bit suspicious. Thomas didn't vote for me and I didn't want to cause problems if he stayed in, so, I just tried to avoid a possible issue.'

He takes another swig of his drink, I follow suit.

'Well, he's gone now, thank goodness, so let's push on.' Claire says, in a way that suggests she is the foreperson of the jury.

'Now, Avon may not have as much insight, as he was with Thomas. What about you Alex? You were with Agatha and Desmond, yes?' she says, clearly taking charge.

'Yes,' Alex says, 'they both seemed real enough.' Claire purses her lips, not satisfied with the response.

'Okay, well, out of the two, who would you guess to be a robot?'

'Well, if I had to choose, I would probably say Agatha. Des was like a typical joyboy. You know, handsome, new money, chasing skirt. He was constantly trying to impress us. It seemed all too real. I don't think they'd spend all that money to make a robot in that image.'

'I agree,' says Claire, 'from what I saw, he seemed more interested in finding romance. Is everyone okay to discount Desmond at this point?'

We all consider it but nod in agreement.

'Okay, so Agatha is a maybe. What about you Kay, what was Elizabeth like?'

'Er, she was…quite a nice lady, we talked about needlework mainly. She was quite reticent, but I never got the impression she was, you know, a robot.'

Claire isn't satisfied.

'For now, we'll call it a maybe. Cliff, who were you with?'

'I was with Amelia. I think she's real. She had a good sense of humour.' I offer. 'Another maybe?'

I stop her there.

'No. We studied each other for a bit. I looked at her face and hands. I don't think she's a robot.' Claire seems unhappy but goes on.

'Okay, Viola?'

'I was with Clem, she kept going on about her success. She was a bit annoying to be honest. Also, she has a peculiar gait when running.'

'I noticed that earlier, when we all ran for the lift.' Avon chips in.

Claire strokes her hair roughly and uses a hair clip to hold it in position.

'Well, I was with Teddy,' she says, 'a poker player who kept showing me his bracelet. Apparently, you get a bracelet if you win a big poker match in Vegas. Likeable but not the sharpest tool in the box. I wouldn't trust him to find his way out of a children's maze. I don't think he's a robot, he seems…too stupid.'

I hope they're not watching us debate in another room. That was a vicious assessment, poor bloke. Poker though, hopefully I'll get a chance to talk to him about the bracelet. You only get one if you win an event in the world series, I'm sure there's a story. Also, if he's winning a bracelet he can't be that stupid, you can't run deep in a game like that on luck alone, you have to have something going on upstairs.

'Right,' says Claire, 'it looks like we're leaning towards Agatha and Clem, any objections?' Nobody seems confident but no objections are called.

'Well then, Avon, go and press the button.' Claire says.

Avon looks embarrassed. For her. What did her last servant die of? Exhaustion? 'We've only just got here?' Alex says.

Claire gives her a sharp look.

Avon, like the rest of us, says nothing and nervously strides across the room. She's certainly in charge.

'I'll just press it then?' he says meekly. 'Yes!' she orders.

He presses it, returns the box button to the table and strolls back to his place. Everyone's quiet, waiting for Claire to take the lead. I hope they vote for her, she's a bit domineering.

'I'll spend a penny,' Claire stands up and turns to Kay, 'hold my drink for me.'

Kay takes her drink, clearly irked. Claire confidently walks to the loo. I look at Avon and raise my eyebrows.

'We've all been naughty.' he grins.

Everyone else has noticed Claire's demonstrative ways and we share looks. 'She's hard work.' Alex says.

'Bloody battle-axe.' Kay agrees.

The main door opens and shuts hastily as Doc comes flying into the room and stands before us. 'The decision is made?' he says.

'Yes.' says Alex. Doc glances around. 'Where's Claire?'

'She's in the bathroom.' says Kay.

Doc considers this news in his usual, theatrical manner, eventually deciding on 'we'll wait.'

He perches on the arm of a sofa and rubs his forehead, as if taking a moment before slipping back into character. We're all getting a peek behind the curtain. He seems oblivious to us being right there. We look nervously amongst ourselves.

It's like being backstage at a talent show.

Finally, we hear the toilet flush and Claire walks out into the room. Doc stands and straightens himself, ready for the next performance. Claire takes her seat, followed by her drink.

'Okay. Who are the two people you have selected?' he asks. 'We have chosen Agatha and Clemence.' Claire says.

'Okay,' he says, 'the other group have selected Avon and Claire, so if the two of you can follow me, I will return with further instructions.'

Avon sips from his pint and stands, Claire looks shocked and shares her disbelief with the rest of the group, by way of looking, well, shocked. We all try to mimic the expression back to her but it's half-hearted at best. They follow Doc out of the room.

'Well, well.' says Kay, struggling to contain her pleasure.

'They picked her, maybe she upset a few of them?' Viola says.

'Well, she is quite forceful,' I say, 'I don't know if she's a robot though?'

'I don't think it's quite so important at this stage. People seem to be voting for who they dislike.' says Viola.

'I wonder if Teddy influenced the decision, he was with her, wasn't he. Maybe it was genuine? Maybe he saw something?' says Alex.

'Yeah but he voted with her last time, he chose Thomas.' I say. 'Maybe he didn't want to choose her while she was there.' says Kay.

Maybe. I wonder what Amelia said about me? It couldn't have been too bad because I wasn't picked. I wonder what happens next? Right on cue, Doc returns, racing through the door like a whirling dervish.

'Okay, the other group have been informed and the pieces are in place. The last thing to do before we go any further is for you to choose, as a group, who to save, Avon or Claire. Who you save will rejoin you for the final decision.'

'Avon.' Kay says immediately. 'Yeah, Avon.' Alex agrees.

Viola nods along, as do I. Doc is satisfied.

'Let's make our way back to the entrance hall and rejoin the clan. We're making very good time. Dinner won't be far away!'

Doc goes to race off.

'What about our drinks!' shouts Alex, as Doc exits through the door. 'Bring them!'

The four of us quickly make our way along the corridor, through the entrance hall and back into the bizarre medical unit, struggling to keep our drinks from spilling at any moment.

Hendon appears from nowhere and firmly shuts the door behind us. Everybody is here. Claire looks furious. Doc looks calm and calculated, despite legging it about all the time. The room settles down.

'Okay, this is what happens. The two groups have chosen to save Agatha and Avon. Agatha and Avon will go to the back of the room and decide between the two of them, who is the robot, Claire or Clemence. The decision is now in their hands. Please go and discuss it now.'

Agatha and Avon walk over to the sliding door, where Hendon stands in earshot.

They begin to have a rather stilted conversation in hushed voices. Everyone in the room watches them, the atmosphere is palpable. A minute passes. They are clearly struggling and fully aware that everyone is waiting with bated breath. They seem to be in agreement, they both look to Doc, who assumes they have reached their verdict.

'Who is the robot?' he says.

They glance at each other again, briefly. Avon speaks. 'Claire.'

Claire lets out a nasty sounding noise, evidently repulsed. 'Claire, you are the suspect, please come to the gurney.'

Claire gives everyone a look of contempt, pure evil. She especially lets Teddy have it. Shaking her head and snarling, her features growing large, very unpleasant.

She rolls her sleeve up and Alex F wastes no time taking a sample. Again, it looks like blood. It's in and out of the machine, Doc makes some notes and delivers the news we're all expecting. 'Incorrect. Claire is human. Hendon will escort you to your driver and your belongings, please.' he says to her.

'Thanks.' she says sarcastically, making sure everyone can taste her displeasure. Hendon follows her out of the main door and shuts it behind him.

'Twelve become eleven!' Doc says, trying to rouse the troops.
'Dinner yet?' says Desmond.

'Not yet, old boy! Soon!'

Doc punts back to the sliding door.

'Now, off to the lift! We're going up to the second floor! Follow me!'

Doc sprints out of view. Somewhat reluctantly, we all follow. I look over at Alex (the one who works here), she is writing up paperwork and not showing any interest in what the rest of us are doing. She takes a screwdriver from the drawer of the desk and lays it on the surface, staring at it like she's unsure what to do next. Maybe she's a robot?

I'm last into the lift and cram in with the others. Doc presses the buttons this time and we ascend. My eyeline is roughly fixed on Avons neck. It looks real, unsurprisingly.

The doors open, revealing another illustriously decorated corridor. To the right of the elevator, an archway leads into a huge, drinking saloon. Tables and chairs fill the room and a sturdy looking bar runs the length. There's a pool table, slot machines, an old donkey derby and a retro jukebox, flashing neon pinks and blues. Doc wanders into the room, Hendon appears from behind the bar, cleaning an empty glass with a bar towel. It almost seems normal.

'Here we are, a chance to relax! Hendon will take any drinks orders, we have most things, there's peanuts and pork scratchings! On the bar, you'll see the red button. This time, you will come to the decision as a group. When you have made your decision, press the button and I will come! Enjoy yourselves, have a game of pool, listen to the jukebox! This is an open vote, we'll go through the motions, after which, dinner!'

Doc looks triumphant and quickly removes himself from sight.

Desmond heads to the bar and starts taking everyone's orders, relaying them to Hendon, who begins readying them with his blank expression. The guests are grouping together, using familiarity as their glue. Amelia approaches.

'This is a bit awkward? Choosing the robot, you know, right in front of them?' She smiles nervously, I smile nervously back.

'What say we get drinks, play pool and discuss? You must have a story about Avon?' she says. 'Not really,' I say, 'he's one of the normal ones. Besides, the pool table is occupied.'

Agatha and Teddy are already racking up, Alex and Desmond

are carrying drinks over, they've monopolised it.

'Donkey derby?' she says.

'Okay,' I say, 'I'm not getting a drink though, I'll end up hammered.' She smiles. 'That's robot talk.'

We approach the bar and order, the others seem to be chatting, with the exception of Avon, who stands alone, sipping a pint.

Amelia has ordered two pints of Guinness, which are placed in front of us. 'Drink up Cliff, it'll line the stomach,' she says, 'hey Avon, donkey derby?' He smiles, 'Alright then.'

The three of us walk to the machine. It doesn't have a slot for money. I guess we just back our horse by pressing the corresponding button. As we place our drinks down, it's clear that Amelia isn't here for the game. The three of us stand in close proximity.

'So Avon,' she says, 'you were with Thomas and he's out, you just survived last time and kicked Claire out, you could say you're fortunate to still be here. What are you thinking now?'

Avon looks around the room and rubs his chin. 'I'm not sure.'

'What about the youngsters playing pool?'

'Well, I've only spoken with Agatha, she did do a weird, jolt…thing.' 'What?'

'You know like when you're going to sneeze but you don't sneeze. It was like that. She didn't acknowledge it though.' he says.

Amelia seems thoughtful. Clemence walks up to us.

'I just wanted to say, no hard feelings. We all have to vote, don't we?' she says. She seems in good fettle.

'I was just saying to Elizabeth and Kay, I've got a property in Switzerland, me and my husband have just returned from there. Lovely place. Anyway, he read an article that said that they've invented some kind of A.I machine that can look at a brain scan and tell you what the brain was looking at! I think he said it was a giraffe. The person looked at a giraffe while they did a brain scan and then they fed it into a machine and the machine said it was a giraffe! And they're building something that can tell you what dreams you had in the night so when you wake up, you ask the machine and it tells you! It's no wonder none of us can tell who the robot is. It's amazing what they're doing these days! We went to a convention a few months ago in Sicily, we've got a property out there, a lovely place, we saw a seminar on robots and all that.

Unbelievable. My husband loves all that, I don't really understand most of it but, it's fascinating!' She stops for air. The three of us take a figurative step back. Amelia seizes the opportunity. 'Did you see Agatha acting weird earlier, when you were with Claire and Avon, when you were waiting for a decision?'

Clem thinks.

'No? She seemed nice?'

Maybe Avon is playing us, trying to throw us off his scent? Or maybe Clem genuinely didn't see it. Amelia ploughs on.

'So who do you think the robot is?' Clem thinks again, taking in the room.

'Okay. I've just spoken with Kay, Elizabeth and Viola, they all seem fine to me, I don't think it's one of them.'

We all look at the crowd around the pool table. They're currently deep in conversation at the far end. Each of them occasionally glance over at us.

'What are they up to?' Avon says. 'Plotting.' Amelia replies. Clem continues.

'Agatha seems okay to me, I haven't spent much time with the others, although I've heard a few things about Teddy, I think he's a bit suspicious.'

'How so?'

'Claire was telling me about him and I don't think it adds up. He doesn't seem like the sort of person who would contribute to this kind of endeavour.'

'I suspect most of us would fall into that category, what about us three?' Amelia says. Claire eyes the three of us.

'I don't really know you yet. You seem okay,' she says to Amelia, 'I think Avon's a nice man, I'm not sure about you though.' she says to me.

'Yeah, he is weird.' Amelia says, teasing me with pleasure. 'I'm not weird,' I say, 'she's pulling your leg.'

Clem smiles nervously. Avon nudges me and gestures towards the pool table. The other two notice and we all look. The four people playing pool, Agatha, Alex, Desmond and Teddy, are creeping quietly into the toilets together. The door shuts behind them. We look quizzically at each other, noticing that the three other ladies have noticed as well. Now the seven of us look bemused.

'What are they doing now?' Avon asks.

'I have no idea?' Viola calls from the other table.

We stare at the door as seconds become minutes. Eventually, Amelia speaks, loud enough for everyone to hear.

'You should check it out.'

I look at her to realise she's directing that question at me. 'Why me?' I say.

'Well, you'd fit in with that crowd, you're…vibrant?' 'Are you asking if I'm vibrant?'

'No, you seem, well, you seem… just go and do it.' 'Yeah, go on Cliff!' Kay says, full of encouragement.

A few of the others weigh in. I concede. I take a gulp of Guinness, exaggerate a head shake and march to the toilets. Christ knows what's going on. I swing the door open and it shuts behind me with purpose. I can be sure I've made enough noise to make my arrival known, in case they really are up to no good.

'Who's that?' I hear a voice ask, maybe Alex.

'Cliff,' I reply, 'what are you lot up to?' I say, in my most liberal sounding voice. Desmond appears before me, looking quite drunk.

'Come on.' he says, escorting me into the main area with a friendly arm over my shoulder. Maybe they're doing cocaine. Maybe I've gone to the real party.

The other three are standing in front of the cubicles. Teddy holds in his hand a pint glass, the contents of which are peculiar and look disgusting. Desmond removes his arm and takes the pint glass from Teddy. He holds it aloft, as if he's won a trophy, looks at me, and says something I was hoping he wouldn't.

'We've had an idea.'

I look at the glass. The contents appear white and sticky. It fills maybe a fifth of the receptacle. It's concerning. I look at Desmond and his watery eyes.

'What is that?' I ask.

'Spunk.' he says, matter of factly.

Teddy bursts into laughter. The ladies look disgusted.

'Desmond!' Alex says.

He smiles at Teddy, who is still laughing. Desmond straightens up. 'Sorry Cliff, it's spit. Not much better, I know.'

'So crude.' Agatha says, nearly smiling.

'We've had an idea, it's highly unlikely that they've taught a robot how to spit. So we've come in here with an empty pint glass,'

'Nearly.' Teddy corrects him.

'A nearly empty pint glass, and we've all done a spit in it so we don't think the robot is one of us.' he says.

I look at the others who nod in agreement, even Alex, who seems appalled by the ordeal. 'Then you walked in.' Teddy says.

Desmond raises his eyebrows and offers me the glass. I look around again, they all seem interested.

'Is this a wind up?' I say.

'No. I know it's rank but it's the best idea we've got right now,' Alex says, 'so if you want to prove you're not…'

It hangs in the air. I reluctantly take the glass and begin to form a liquid in my mouth. 'You all saw each other do it?' I ask.

They all nod. I hold the glass six inches below my mouth and gozz into it. 'Well done Cliff, you passed!' Desmond says, taking the glass from me. 'What now?' Alex asks.

'Well,' I say, 'we all noticed you lot coming in here, so everyone else is waiting for me to go out there and explain what you're doing.'

'Do you need a piss?' says Desmond. 'No?' I say.

'So you were the canary?' he says. 'I guess.'

'Well, that's five of us, if we can get one more person to do this, we'll have the majority vote and we'll be able to swing it. Then we can have dinner. Shall we all go out there and offer it up?' Desmond says, lifting the glass.

'I think we should keep that glass on the back burner Des, it's not going to help persuade anyone to do anything.' says Agatha.

'Alright, alright. Lead the way mate.' he says to me.

I look for assurance from the others and walk out first. Maybe they'll shut the door behind me and feed me to the wolves. They don't, and the five of us queue up next to the pool table, similar to a police suspect line-up. Desmond keeps the glass by his side. The other six watch us from down the room, even Hendon is paying attention. Nobody says anything so I step out of the line and begin.

'They've had an idea.' I say, awkwardly unsure as to how to deliver the idea to the others. They wait patiently.

'Basically, when I went in there…' I'm struggling to explain.

Unfortunately for everyone, Desmond has noticed and is strutting into the centre of the room, glass aloft. I'm hoping he doesn't announce it in the same way that he did to me. That kind of joke wouldn't fly out here. Already, upon noticing the glass, a few of them look mortified. 'Basically, we agreed that it's highly unlikely that they've made a robot that can spit. So we went to the toilet and all spit into this glass.' he shows them the evidence proudly. They react as if he's showing them a severed head.

'So we figure, if you can spit, you're probably not the robot. We all did it. Cliff came in and did it. Who's in?'

They're looking at me with disdain. Except for Amelia, who

comes striding towards us, takes the glass from Desmond and spits into it with conviction. She passes it back to Desmond, walks to the bar and Hendon takes her order.

'Who's next?' he says, waving it about inappropriately.

I watch as Viola, then Avon, step up and do the deed. They join Amelia at the bar, as do Teddy, Agatha and Alex. Desmond and I are left to judge the ordeal.

'Well?' he says.

'I'm not doing that, it's abhorrent.' says Elizabeth. 'Well eight of us have done it, so we'll have the vote.' 'I don't care, it's disgusting.' she says.

'What about you two?' Desmond asks. Clemence and Kay are clearly not keen. 'No, I don't think so.' Kay says.

'Look, prove it's not you. This idea is as good as we've got right now. It's rank but we've all done it, as soon as you do it, we can vote and go and have dinner. We can act civilised and pretend this didn't happen.' Desmond probes.

They all seem reluctant. Clemence heads over sheepishly and does it as privately as possible but it's verifiable. She looks at the other two shamefully before heading to the bar. Everyone there is watching from a safe distance.

'So?' Desmond exhorts.

Elizabeth and Kay aren't forthcoming.

'I'm not doing it, sorry.' Elizabeth says firmly. Kay sighs.

'Fine.'

She begrudgingly paces to us, takes the glass as if she's handling evidence and with clear embarrassment, spits into the glass. Immediately, Desmond walks to the bar and presses the button.

'What are you doing?' Agatha asks.

'Getting Doc here. We're all voting for Elizabeth. That's the game.' he sounds assured.

It's more complicated than that but he's right. Nobody is arguing, not even Elizabeth. I wonder if she is the robot. This could all be over and we could enjoy a nice dinner and we'd all get a prize, that'd be nice. What if she isn't the robot though? The game continues, they've built a robot that can spit and we're all gonna keep drinking. I must stop, I'm beginning to feel it.

Desmond is ordering another one, it's free and he's taking full advantage. It reminds me of a wedding, where you end up getting really drunk with people who aren't that familiar to you. The door opens and Doc approaches the bar.

'You rang!' he says, in a classic butler cliche voice.

'We're done.' Desmond says, drinking about half of his pint in one go. Blimey.

'That was relatively quick, if you're all ready then,' Doc says, 'I shall take your vote.'

'No need to build up the drama, we're all voting for Elizabeth, right?' Desmond asks around the room. No objections ring out.

'Right.' Elizabeth says.

'Right,' Doc says, 'to the elevator!' He gallops off.

'What shall we do with our drinks?' Agatha calls but he's already out of earshot.

'Bring it.' Avon says, starting after him.

We all race to the elevator and begin cramming in. Hendon has followed the mob and waits until everyone else is set. It's still a tight squeeze.

'There isn't enough room Hendon, take the stairs.' Doc says

curtly.

Hendon lets out a barely noticeable snort, but his expression remains unchanged. He disappears from view before the doors slide shut for our descent.

The moments in the lift are uncomfortable. An awkward silence falls. Even Doc is statuesque. We all wait for the doors to open and finally they do. We follow Doc across the entrance hall and once again, gather in the unit.

Elizabeth promptly waits next to the gurney for Alex to administer the needle. She seems accepting of the decision, if somewhat saddened by the approach. Alex takes a sample and inserts it into the computer. The moment of truth. I don't know about the others but for me, this is the first time it feels like a proper guess. I think the other two evictions were personal selections, this one feels different. Doc eyes the results and turns to the group.

'Negative,' he says, 'another human.' Most of us look surprised.

'I'm afraid the night is over for you Elizabeth; Hendon will escort you out.' Doc says.

'Well, I'm a bit annoyed actually. It's been an awful experience and I won't be donating in the future.' she says.

'I'm sorry you feel that way, still, the show must go on.' Doc says in an aloof manner, gesturing her towards the exit. Quite rude.

Elizabeth raises her eyebrows.

'Wow.' she says, striding out of the door, clearly offended. Hendon follows.

'Well, there we are,' Doc says, 'you can't please everyone, try as you might. We will go to the dining room now and enjoy supper. I'm sure some of you would appreciate food in your belly. Come!'

Doc ships through the sliding door and away. We've spent a lot of time chasing him around so far. Desmond leans into me as we bounce along the entrance hall and down a different corridor. 'This'll be interesting. Robots don't eat, do they.'

It's a fair point but before I can respond he speeds up and starts talking to Alex. I see Doc enter a door on the left and people begin to filter in. I reach the door and enter a huge dining room.

Once again, expensive items are paraded everywhere, all accompanying a long, polished dining table. Each place is set up with a cacophony of splendour. There are twelve seats around the table and each place has a name card folded in half, so it stands up in front of the seat. 'Welcome to the dining room, please take your seat, Hendon will arrive with drinks shortly.' Doc says, swinging into the seat at the head of the table, nearest the door.

I glance at the nametag; it says his name on it so fair enough. The others look for their name tags and take their places. Agatha and Amelia study different paintings on either side of the room. Both are twentieth century works, I recognise them. They're excellent pieces, though thought-provoking and terrifying, not suitable for a dining room really. I find my place at the far end of the table.

On one side is the other head of the table, directly next to me is Desmond. He's interesting, if nothing else. I lean over to see the name at the head. It's Alex Forrester, so I guess the scientist woman is joining us. I don't fear her talking my ear off.

A side door opens and Hendon walks in carrying six bottles of wine, minus the class and elegance of a trained waiter. He has three bottles in each hand and he plonks them on the table without grace. Next, he uses a bottle opener from the table and extracts the corks expertly, in fairness. Several of us are watching him, including Doc, who is obviously not impressed with his manner. Hendon goes around the table, filling the two glasses in front of every place with one colour of each. Desmond immediately takes the red and demolishes it.

'Again,' he says.

Hendon does so. He then pours mine. I thank him after each one but he doesn't acknowledge. When finished, he picks up the empty bottles and skulks off. Doc uses a knife on a glass to gain attention. Agatha and Amelia are still standing but turn to him.

'First of all, well done for making it to dinner! During our previous encounters before tonight, I'm aware that Amelia, Clemence and Cliff do not eat meat, so a wonderful alternative has been prepared. Secondly, you may have noticed the transparent box in the centre of the table. Alex will arrive shortly with pens and paper. Each of you will cast your vote by writing the name of your suspect on the piece of paper. I would then ask you to ball it up and place it into the box. Only when all ten of you have done so, will the results be announced. This is blind vote, discussing it is allowed of course but your decision must be your own.'

Alex F enters the room with pens and paper and sets them down on a cabinet just inside the door. She closes the door and quietly scuttles to her seat at the top of the table. I offer her a smile and she manages one back. Sort of.

'Here she is!' Doc announces. 'You may vote from now onwards!'

Nobody is paying attention. We have such stylish and tasteful silverware in front of us, that it's a surprise when Hendon reappears with a stack of takeaway pizzas. He plants them on the table in two piles, opens a box, takes a slice and stands in front of the closed entry door, attacking it. Doc takes a couple of slices onto his plate and passes them along. Everyone helps themselves in turn. Amelia sits next to Doc, Agatha takes her place next to Desmond and so begins their dance. There's something going on there.

As the food reaches our end, Viola, who is opposite me, is deep in conversation with Kay, her neighbour. Desmond passes me the pizza boxes without looking, smitten with Agatha. I dig out two slices of the vegetarian variety and pass them on to Alex F.

'No thanks.' she says, engrossed on her phone.

I pass them across to Viola, who accepts with a courteous smile.

I tuck in and quickly notice Viola and Kay watching closely from across the table. They must be watching me eat and I become aware how important this is. A look around the table confirms that everyone is tucking in, with the exception of Avon, who has taken three slices but hasn't started on them. Viola meets my gaze, making sure I'm watching as she takes a generous bite. Kay has also indulged. Avon is on my side, up the other end, next to Doc. I don't have a good view, what with Agatha and Desmond cavorting between us. The other seat on this side, next to Avon, is Alex. It currently sits vacant, as Alex is over by Hendon, casting her vote at the cabinet. Already.

She balls up her paper, walks back to the table, sits down and puts it in the box. She doesn't look up, she just carries on eating.

The other people seem oblivious but Viola, Kay and I saw. Doc saw it too. I look at Alex F, who is doom scrolling on her phone. She isn't eating. Maybe she's a robot. She must sense something and looks up at me.

'What?'

'Nothing,' I say, then it comes to me. 'Well, do you know who the robot is?' She looks pensive.

'Yeah.'

'Any tips?' I say.

'No.' she says, returning to her phone.

Fair enough. That told me. My eyes wander back up the table. Avon, who still hasn't started eating, is up at the cabinet, voting. A few of the others are watching him. He's taking his sweet time. I clap eyes on Clemence, who looks baffled. Viola is watching, filled with uncertainty. Doc is smiling, enjoying the confusion. And the food.

Avon returns to the table and posts his balled-up paper into the box. It's transparency revealing two votes, no funny business. Just to add to the bewilderment, he picks up a large slice of pizza, and certain that all eyes are on him, takes two abundant mouthfuls.

I grab another slice and start to worry about who I'm going to vote for.

Chapter Three
The Dilemma.

This is a dilemma. In some respects, I've managed to avoid voting thus far, however, this time there's no getting around it. Everyone here can eat, drink and spit. As I eat a second slice I begin to work along the table, starting on my right. Desmond.

I don't think it's Desmond although he is a bit much.

He and Agatha stand, he downs another glass of wine and they walk towards the cabinet. He pats her behind in a playful way, she clearly enjoyed the affection. Together they begin to write their votes. Perhaps one convinced the other on who to vote for. Evidently they don't seem too worried about the ramifications. They saunter back to the table and put them in the box. That's four.

I don't think it's Agatha either. I think her and Des are young and wealthy and here to have fun. The next seat is Alex. She voted first. I haven't really spoken with her so I haven't had a chance to assess the land. She's a maybe.

On the end is Avon. Also voted. I like him, though I think he's got a few of them suspicious. Maybe a tactical vote if I had no reason to vote for anyone else…but I like him. I'd vote Alex over him.

Doc sits at the end, looking pleased with himself, decimating the pizza. He hasn't stopped since he started. I turn to Alex F.

'Where's the toilet.'

She looks up from the phone and points to the far corner, where Hendon brought the food and drink out.

'Thanks.' I say but she has already returned to the black mirror.

I walk through the door and into a small pantry room. There is a fridge and a dumb waiter over the top of a small cupboard. I open the cupboard door and have a nose inside. A few old cloths and a sponge.

Off of the room is another door, which opens into a tiny lavatory. Just enough room to do your business. I do my business, wash my hands and rejoin the others. I wonder if anyone else has voted.

Looking at the glass box, I'm not really sure. When I sit back down and pick up my glass of white, (the red will definitely give me a hangover, regardless of the amount I drink),

Viola leans in. 'Amelia voted.'

My eyes widen briefly, to show that I heard her. I taste the wine, place it down and continue my thoughts.

Amelia. I'm not voting for Amelia. Robot or not, I like Amelia. I'm not ready to burn that bridge. Next to her is Teddy, who is currently engaged in conversation with Clem, in the next seat. She's talking his face off and he's visibly disconnected. Occasionally smiling politely and nodding when Clem stops for air. I haven't spoken with either in great length but I don't get the impression that either are what I'm looking for. Still, they both go in the maybe pile with Alex.

That leaves Kay and Viola. Again, I haven't got to know either, but they have paired up somewhat. Both seem to be playing the game, watching other guests closely for any sign or hiccup. It wouldn't be the worst idea for a robot to pair up with someone and cast aspersions about everyone else.

I drink my wine and decide that Teddy is safe. I'd like to talk with him about poker and he seems quite affable. I would vote for Clemence but it would be based on her self-involved droning rather than her automated qualities. Still, she stays in the hat.

I watch Kay and Viola again, still watching everyone like hawks and then sharing their opinions with each other. I decide to get involved.

'Hey.' I say gently.

They stop and stare at me.

'I noticed that neither of you have voted yet, what are you thinking?' I say. Viola leans on the table, taking charge.

'We're thinking of voting the same, you know, to increase the chances of that person leaving. We've narrowed it down to three.'

'How do you mean, leaving? Shouldn't we be finding the bot?'

'You know as well as I do, that some people here are just plain annoying. It's a fine balancing act between choosing the one who you think is a robot or the one who you can't bear to be around for another moment.' she says.

Viola speaks bluntly but it's true. I mean, Thomas was kicked out for being a bellend. No other reason.

'So, who's the three?' I ask.

They share a look and Kay leans in too.

'If we tell you, would you consider voting the same way as well?' she says. 'I would.' I say carefully.

Viola leans even closer to me. I lean closer as well. It's a bit clandestine.

'We're thinking Teddy, Clemence or you. Obviously, if you're in, we'll go the other way.'

'Why me?' I say, as casually as I can muster. Viola lowers her tone even further.

'You turned up late, you eat funny, you drink slowly, but if you're in, WE'LL GO THE OTHER WAY.'

The three of us sit back in a normal position as if nothing happened. Glancing about confirms we're not being watched. It's very covert. I don't want to be out if they're wary of me.

'I'm in,' I nod, 'how do we choose out of the other two?'
'What do you think of them?' Kay asks me.

'Well,' I say, 'I haven't talked to either in great length, I know Clem has a tendency to go on about herself and other people have commented on Teddy but, they both seem…not the robot? What do you two know about them?'

Viola leans forward again.

'The word is that Teddy won his money playing poker. Now I'll tell you three things about poker that make me very suspicious. Number one, you win some big money playing poker, millions, however, it's maybe not in the person's mentality for contributing to a venture like this. Number two, I talked to him earlier about poker, he's wearing a bracelet. You can run lucky in a game for a long time but in order to win a bracelet you have to run lucky for days, not hours. For that amount of time, at some point, you're gonna have to lean on your skill. It's inevitable. He didn't know the odds of pocket nines versus ace king off, preflop. I played poker for two years in college and I'll tell you now, it's easier to play when you know the maths. I don't believe in his skill. Number three. Talking in general, he seems like someone who hasn't made his own way. Dare I say, his intelligence is low and his childish adolescence is high. His backstory doesn't match his personality and I question his success and therefore, his authenticity.'

Wow. She seems to have his number; she seems very certain. Kay looks ambivalent. 'What about Clem?' I say.

We stop talking and watch Teddy walk over to the cabinet. He looks nervously at the rest of us before casting his vote, clearly debating over the decision. He walks back to the table, posts his screwed-up paper and disappears to the toilet. Clem has engaged with Kay and bangs on about eating octopus in Peru. Viola leans back to me and gestures me forward. We're talking about Clem so we're having to be even more covert.

'She's malleable.' 'What?' I say.

'I think we can attain her cooperation.' 'What, with the voting?'

Viola nods to Kay and Clem. We eavesdrop as the conversation is steered by Kay into voting. Viola quickly jumps into the chat and starts indicating that their desire is to vote for Teddy. Clem explains that she already has her own suspicions regarding Teddy and before you can say "Let's all vote for Teddy," the two of them get up and approach the cabinet together. As they leave, Viola gives Kay and I a look. Kay moves from her chair into Viola's chair, opposite me.

'Don't trust her. She's hellbent on finding the robot.' she says. 'Well that's the game.' I say, smiling.

'I know but it's strange, she's too, I don't know, she seems intent on directing suspicion from herself, she won't entertain the idea that anyone thinks it's her, it's making me uncomfortable.' 'I thought you two were as thick as thieves?'

'She won't leave me alone; she's latched onto me. She basically directs me on who to vote for. She's over there with Clem, forcing her to vote whichever way she wants.'

'She's hardly forcing her…but I can see your point. What's your plan?'

Clem has cast her vote, under the watchful gaze of Viola. Viola hasn't voted but they both head back to the table. Clem puts her vote into the box and sits down. Kay has shifted back to her own chair and Viola sits across from me.

'We're the only people left to vote.' Viola says, with an almost satisfied glee. Kay is right, there's something odd about her, she's a bit demonstrative.

'Clemence voted for Teddy, I saw it happen. If the three of us vote for him, he'll have four. The little birds tell me that Des and Agatha will vote for him so that'll be enough. Are you ready?' Viola asks us.

Kay gives me a quick glance as she stands and sets off towards the cabinet, subordinately. 'Wait here.' Viola says to me, as she follows Kay.

I contemplate the decision. Clem is sipping her wine, dejection across her face. How can I trust that they're voting for him, they might be voting for me? Mind you, Viola is hovering over Kay as she writes, the same as she did to Clemence, and Clemence was openly discussing her reasoning behind a possible vote for Teddy. She glances over at me, then quickly away, filling me with doubt. I'm not sure what to do. I look at Doc, who has finished with the pizza and is enjoying the chaotic atmosphere around him, flexing his fingers and displaying a shit-eating grin.

Kay and Viola return to their seats. Viola looks determined. Kay looks crestfallen. 'Are you ready?' Viola asks me.

I squirm in my seat but bravely challenge her. 'How come you haven't voted yet?'

It's her turn to squirm.

'Because for this plan to work, I'm ensuring that we're all doing the same thing.'

'Are you worried that you'll vote, then the rest of us will do something different?' I say. 'No,' she snaps, 'I'm just making sure we're all on the same page.'

'Are you the self-appointed leader then?' She leans towards me, full of menace.

'I want that prize. I need that prize. Stick with me and you'll go far. Defy me and you will be destroyed. No more fun and games. I'm not a robot. I intend to find out who is. Now come with me over there, we'll both vote for him, then we can strategize the next move.'

'How do you know?' I say firmly. 'How do I know what?'

'How do you know you're not a robot?' 'I just know.'

'But they could have implanted you with a past, a memory of who you are, you can't know.' Viola's eyes sadden.

'I've been through some…tough things recently. Health…death…they wouldn't be cruel enough to implant this history into a robot. They couldn't…I'm not a robot. I just know.'

She seems genuinely sorrowful. Verging on tears. A big change in her usual, stoic manner. I lean towards Viola, feeling somewhat bad for her.

'I'll vote for him, I'm on it.'

She offers me a smile. I stand and march to the cabinet, alone.

As I take the lid off of the pen, a moment of uncertainty washes over me. I look back at the group. Most of them are chatting amongst themselves. Kay and Viola are both watching me intently. Despite the question mark I have over Viola, I will keep my word and vote for Teddy. If fortunate enough to survive this vote, I will purposefully distance myself from her in future. I'm not keen on her tactics or her personality.

I scribble his name on the piece of paper, screw it up and walk back to the table. Amelia, Teddy, Clemence and Avon are all watching me as I post my vote and sit down. Viola is still looking downcast. As is Kay. Doc, on the other hand is cock a hoop, shaking with excitement and anticipation.

'One left!' he shouts, catching most of us off guard.

All eyes turn toward Viola. A cynic might suggest she's enjoying the control. 'You ready?' Kay says gently.

Viola nods, exuding a desperate emotional state. Two minutes ago she had a monstrous intent. Now she acts like someone with a difficult decision to make. I don't like this at all. She shuffles to the cabinet, aware that everyone is burning eyes into her. She scrawls a name on the paper, moves back to the table and posts it. Before she's even sat down, Doc springs up and collects the box in the centre of the table.

'It's done!' he exclaims, sitting back at the head of the table and shaking the box, presumably to mix up the entries. Everyone is sitting down and watching Doc, in a similar way to when you watch a child unwrap their Christmas presents.

'Okay then,' he says, 'I will read out the votes in the unit downstairs. Leave your drinks, we will return here afterwards, come!'

Doc races from the room in the style that we've come to accept. There is a particularly slow procession following him, the food and drink have taken their toll. Even Hendon drags his heels. We do the lift, without his presence. He takes the stairs, three at a time.

When I reach the unit, I stand with the group who have already arrived and wait for the stragglers. Doc and Alex F take their places by the gurney. The last of the gang pile in and Hendon slides the door closed behind them. Doc places the transparent box on the gurney and addresses the crowd.

'Here we go then, I'll stop, if and when a decision is reached.' An eerie silence falls as Doc begins to go through the box.

'Teddy.' he says, reading his initial pick aloud and briefly showing us, to prove he isn't making it up.

It's my vote, I can tell by the handwriting. Doc continues with his method. 'Desmond. Teddy. Desmond. Cliff.'

That's one for me. The boys aren't doing very well. 'Teddy. Clemence. Teddy.'

By my reckoning, Teddy now has four votes and with two votes left to announce, only Desmond can catch him as he has two, the rest of us are safe. Doc continues.

'Teddy.' he reads, immediately putting on a glum expression. 'I'm afraid that's it you old chum, you can't be caught.'

Teddy seems bemused as Alex F takes a sample from his arm and does her computer work with it.

'Anything to say old boy?' Doc asks him, before studying the computer screen. Teddy looks around at us, apparently blindsided by the decision.

'I don't believe it.' he manages. Doc addresses the room.

'Another human! You've missed again, gang! Hendon, will you escort our friend out please, all the best!'

Hendon strides across the room and with a firm hand on his lower back, steers Teddy to the exit. You can tell by the look on his face, Teddy is so surprised that he isn't able to reach other emotions like anger or sadness.

Maybe Viola was right, rigging the vote. Maybe it was his misfortune. The thing now though, is that he was a human, which only increases my distrust of her.

'Single figures now gang! Ten becomes nine!' says our host with the most. 'What happens now?' Avon asks.

'What happens now old boy, is that it's my go! Alex?' Doc rolls up his sleeve and Alex F takes a blood sample.

'I'm sure that some of you think that maybe I'm a robot? My ex-wife would often accuse me of a lack of emotional feelings. Well, hopefully I can allay your fears!'

Alex and Doc monitor the screen and Doc gestures to the screen, inviting us to look and see. I'm nearest so I zone in. I don't understand most of what I'm looking at but blood and sugar levels are normal and all of the measurements are where they should be. He is human. A few of the others are looking at it as well.

He waves the printout around, as if expecting any of us will understand it.

'I'm a human being, if any of you run into my ex-wife, please pass on this information, so she can grow up and stop casting aspersions.'

I sense hostility. He continues.

'I wanted to prove to you that I'm a human and so any

nagging doubts that you have are quashed. We move forward as a nine. Let's head back to the dining room where the next part of our game begins!'

He gallops through the sliding door and into the hall. Everyone follows but nobody is running anymore, that ship has sailed. Alex F and Hendon walk with the rest of us, Doc and his infectious tenacity has been trumped by a total lack of urgency.

Finally, the gang make it back to the dining room, minus Teddy. We all sit in our previous places and continue with our wines. There's still some pizza in the boxes but nobody is partaking. 'Now we come to our next game,' Doc says, 'a trio of fun!'

He looks around the table, hoping his words have landed. We all remain unmoved. Hendon advances to the table and starts to help himself to the pizza.

'Not now, Hendon!'

Doc gives him a steely look. Hendon sheepishly backs away, empty handed. Doc puts the face back on.

'Alex, Hendon and I will wait here. The rest of you will be split into groups of three, once in your group, feel free to roam the halls. Certain doors will be locked but if not, please take in the many delights scattered around. Your job is to bring me one name from another group of three, who you suspect may be the machine. We will all meet back here and once I have the three

names, you will have an open discussion as a group of nine, to debate the selections and from them, make your final accusation. Do you all understand?'

There are no objections. 'Right then, the groups!'

Alex F has walked to Docs side and the two of them

scrutinise the clipboard in hushed voices. The rest of us sit quietly, quaffing wine. Resolved, Alex F sits back down at the other end of the table.

'Right. As there are three boys left, we've split them up, divide and conquer, eh girls!' he says, glancing around the table, an inane grin on his face. No reactions gauged, he continues.

'So, Agatha, Avon and Viola, you're group one. Amelia, Desmond and Clemence, you're group two.'

Amelia scowls at me good-naturedly as I try to return a sympathetic look. It's a pig of a group. Desmond is hammered and Clem is, well, Clem.

'That leaves Alex, Kay and Cliff as group three. You're all free to explore. We'll see you back here when your decision is made!'

Doc walks to the toilet, pleased with his latest performance. Hendon watches him carefully before slowly advancing towards the pizza boxes.

Group one have assembled themselves and are exiting. Agatha is younger than the other two and looks disappointed with the draw. I wonder if Viola will start trying to influence them with her aggression, if she hasn't done so previously.

Clemence is talking with enthusiasm at Amelia, something about Finland. Amelia is glancing nervously across the table at Desmond, who seems to be struggling to get to his feet.

Kay has rounded the table and naturally, the pair of us accost Alex with goodwill. The three of us exit the room, I glance back at Amelia who notices and rolls her eyes comically.

'Shall we go back to the entrance hall or carry on down the way?' Kay says. I don't mind and shrug my shoulders.

'Let's carry on down the way, we haven't been down there

yet.' Alex says.

We walk together, further along the corridor. It turns to the right and has a door on either side. Alex tries one, I try the other but both are locked. We continue walking as there is one more door at the end.

'Do you think Doc lives here?' asks Alex.

'I guess so,' I say, 'he seems to know the lay of the land.'
'What about the other two?'

'Maybe,' I say, 'Hendon probably has his own pantry.' We all laugh.

'Yeah, perhaps Doc lets him sleep at the end of the bed, if he's good.' says Alex. We all laugh again.

The door at the end of the corridor opens into a stairwell. 'Up or down?' Alex asks with a hint of excitement.

'Let's try down?' Kay says.

Alex smiles at both of us and begins down the stairs.

We take two flights to the bottom. HALL TWO is written in capital letters on the wall. A fire exit is on one side, a locked door is on the far wall and a door with a key in the lock is on the internal wall. Alex turns the key and pushes it open.

The three of us enter a darkened room and Alex searches the wall for a light switch. We hear a click when she finds it. The room slowly brightens, revealing a huge, I guess, dancefloor? The room is half the size of a football pitch, complete with a bar, tables and chairs around the side, more ostentatious wall hangings and a DJ booth at the opposite end. It's classy and has an old-fashioned elegance.

'It's a ballroom.' Kay exclaims.

Several disco balls hanging from the ceiling are catching the light and throwing elaborate shapes across the floor, the three of us stand with mouths agape, it's magical.

'Where do you think the others are?' Kay asks, almost unconcerned. 'Who cares.' Alex replies, engrossed in the panorama.

'This place is incredible.' I say.

Alex walks across the floor to the music booth. Kay and I watch her pressing buttons and changing light settings.

'I'm trying to get the music to come on!' she shouts.

She continues mucking around in there, wearing the headphones and looking like a plum. 'We need to talk about Viola.' Kay says to me.

'Yeah. You were interrupted earlier.'

'I just…I just don't trust her. She might be the machine. She's constantly putting ideas in your head and talking about how other people have been doing strange things and basically trying to dictate the votes.'

'She's not trying, she's succeeding. Did you vote for Teddy last time?'

'Of course I did. She was in my personal space, watching what I was writing. I had to. I didn't even mind Teddy, I wasn't suspicious of him. She just got like a dog with a bone about it. I think we should vote for her.'

I'm not a fan of Viola. I give Kay an understanding nod.

'The three of us have to agree on our vote, what about Alex?' I say.

'I'm not sure, I don't think she and Vi have spent much time together, she may not have a problem with voting for her?'

'Unless she suspects someone else and tries to influence us?'
'Have you got to know her?'

'No. You?'

'No.'

'Okay,' I say, 'let's see what she says.'

We walk across the floor together and reach the booth. Alex is still trying to make the magic happen but is only succeeding at messing up the levels for whichever poor soul has to perform here next.

'I can't get it going.' Alex says, sliding the headphones from her ears so that they wrap around her neck. She looks the part.

'We need to talk about tactics.' I say jovially.

'Cool, I could do with going back for another drink anyway.' Alex replies, taking the headphones off completely and hanging them on a well-positioned hook.

The three of us dawdle across the floor, back towards where we came in. 'What are you thinking?' Alex directs the question to me.

'Well, Kay and I were talking about Viola.'

Alex considers this.

'Okay, I see what you're saying, I haven't talked with her much but she seems wary of everyone. I suppose that's pretty natural though, under the circumstances?'

'Her recent behaviour has been quite threatening.' Kay says.

'I agree,' I say, 'she told me she needs to win, she needs the prize, she's had recent troubles, she was quite forceful about it.'

Alex looks between us, thinking it over.

'I don't think the other group will vote for her. She's with Agatha and Avon, his agenda is anyone's guess, but Agatha doesn't go much on Clem so unless Viola has an issue with it, I suspect they'll go that way.'

'She would have an issue with it, she's got Clem in the palm of her hand.' I say. 'So who will they vote for?'

'I think she'll try to get them to go for Desmond, I don't think she likes him.' says Kay. 'Who would? He's unlikely to be a machine though, I mean, you have met him?' Alex is right. Kay continues.

'I think that she thinks if enough of us vote the same way, then jump on the bandwagon and get rid.'

Alex contemplates.

'Okay, so Desmond is with Clem and Amelia. Who will they vote for? I mean, if we can predict who the other two groups vote for, we can use our vote to double up and then there's only two people in the main vote. If you think about it, if we can pick the same person as another group, then it's gonna be easier to convince the others because we'll already be in the majority. Does that make sense?'

Kay looks as confused as me. Alex tries again with a purposeful, almost patronising, slower voice.

'If all three groups choose different people, the remaining people have three to select from. If two groups choose the same person, they'll only be two choices. If us and another group have the same nomination, we'll have the majority and so that person will be likely to go out. Get it?' 'What if all three groups pick the same person?' asks Kay.

'They can't. You can't choose someone from your own group.' I jump in.

'So, if we can predict who the other two groups select, we can make our decision based on that and have the advantage when it comes to selecting the robot in the unit?'

Alex applauds sarcastically but not in a rude way.

'You got it. We've just got to work out who the other groups vote for, whether it's a robot or not. It doesn't matter.'

Kay has the comprehension and is already working on it.

'I think Viola will force her will on Agatha and Avon and get the vote for Desmond.' 'I'm not so sure, Agatha is smitten. I can't see her going for it.'

'I agree,' I say. 'It's more likely she knows this and also, she seemed to know who they were voting for last time, maybe they're in cahoots?'

'Maybe,' says Alex, 'and are you two in cahoots with her as well?' 'For now.' Kay replies.

I look sheepish, Alex keeps thinking aloud.

'So, if we assume that Viola has the control in her group, she has the call over you two in this group and Des and Clem in the other group, it only leaves a vote for Amelia or me.'

'Well, we can't vote for you.' I say.

'So is she gonna force the vote on Amelia?'

'I'm not sure? She hasn't really mentioned Amelia before.' Kay says. 'No, I agree.' I say.

I like Amelia, we smoked together. I don't really want to vote for her.

'If Viola is as wily as you suggest, she might be playing the same way. Who do you think Viola thinks this group will vote for?' Alex asks.

I think. 'Clem?'

'Or Desmond. But Agatha wouldn't do it.' Kay finishes my thought.

'So if she thinks we'd vote for Clem, would she sacrifice her pawn and go the same way? She wouldn't have to press Agatha too hard, and Avon, well Avon is a mystery but he might not stand in the way?'

'Well, Avon voted for me earlier.' I say, looking for sympathy.

'Well, you do have that look about you.' Alex jokes. I think. Kay chuckles. 'Okay, so Clem or Amelia?'

I try diplomacy.

'I don't think she'd go for Amelia; I don't think enough people would vote for her in the final decision, it'd be a wasted vote. Agatha wouldn't be cool about voting for Desmond so Clemence would be the frontrunner.'

Kay reluctantly nods in agreement. Alex debates.

'Do either of you see Des, Amelia and Clem voting for Viola?' she says. Kay and I consider the idea. Alex continues.

'If they do and we do, she'll have problems getting out of it.' 'I don't know who they'll vote for.' Kay ponders.

'Well, if Clem wasn't in the same group, he'd vote for her.' Alex says. 'He didn't last time.' I murmur.

'How do you know?'

'Viola suggested they were voting for Teddy and he got the votes.' 'What do you mean, suggested?'

'She implied that she knew what they'd do.' Alex thinks over the information.

'Well then, they can't vote for Amelia but if she has both of their ears, that group will vote Avon, or me. I'm thinking me.'

'But we can't vote for you, so why would she hedge her bets, you haven't fallen under suspicion?' says Kay.

'This is becoming too complicated, why don't we vote for

Viola, thus ensuring she's in the next vote?' I suggest.

We're standing at the bottom of the stairwell, having made our way across the glamorous ballroom. It's darker and adds to the slander being spouted about.

'We could?' Alex says carefully.

'She wouldn't be happy.' Kay says, worried about the ramifications. 'We're all gonna get voted for, sooner or later?' Alex offers.

'It's that or we vote for Clem. She's been voted for before, there's no doubt that she's been annoying people so she's a likely suspect. That said, I don't think she's a robot.'

After I say it, the three of us look discouraged, unsure as to what to do. 'Let's vote. See where we're at. Clemence or Viola.' Alex says.

We look at each other. Nobody wants to go first. Alex takes the lead. 'I'll vote Viola.' she says.

I think Kay will vote for Clem, she won't pick Viola, she hasn't got the stomach. Then it will be down to me.

'Viola,' Kay says, 'let's do it. Crikey. Well that showed me. 'Okay,' I say, 'Viola.'

'That's it then, let's do it.' Alex says, tackling the stairs.

We follow her up the two flights of stairs and along the corridor. I'm glad she remembers the way; all of this money looks the same to me. She enters the correct door and Kay and I hit the dining room at just the right time.

Desmond is being violently sick into the base of a plant pot. Well, some of it is going into the plant pot, a fair amount is going all over the floor. Everyone else is back in the room so he has a full audience. Some are looking disdainfully at the scene while others are racing around like headless chickens, looking for towels or mops or buckets. Doc stands over him, inspecting the contents. He sees that we have entered and approaches.

'You've made your decision?' he says, acting as if we haven't noticed the utter carnage over his shoulder.

'What's going on.' Kay says, trying to disguise her alarm. 'Desmond has taken a turn.' Replies Doc.

'Taken a turn! He's smashed!' Alex states.

Des has stopped being sick, he's breathing heavily and is oblivious to the situation he finds himself in. In fairness, when you're smashed and being sick, you do have less inhibitions. 'So you have your decision?' Doc inquires.

'We do.' Affirms Alex.

'I have the other votes, please offer yours..' Alex leans into his ear.

'Viola.'

'Very good,' says Doc, 'the announcement is imminent.'

He returns to Desmond, who is using the wall to hold himself up. Hendon and Avon are close by, watching for a slump. Viola looks disgusted by it, I daresay she'll be even more disgusted when she finds her name read out.

Everyone is looking nervously at each other; the distrust is growing by the second. Amelia beelines to me, I smile, pleased to see her.

'We voted for Viola, you?' she says. 'Yeah, Viola.' I say, surprised. 'Interesting! She's gonna be pissed!'

'What's going on with him?' I say, pointing at Desmond, who has collapsed over Avon while Hendon offers them both support. Doc stands in close proximity, grinning.

'He has obviously drunk too much, not the behaviour you'd expect from a robot. So, anyway, if both of our groups voted for Viola, there's only gonna be two people in the vote. Who d'ya think their group voted for?'

'I dunno. Your name was mentioned.' 'What do you mean?'

'We were discussing who they might vote for and your name was mentioned.' Amelia squints her eyes.

'Were you working out who they voted for so you could vote the same way, tactical like?' 'Sort of?' I shrug.

'Firstly, that's very stealthy Cliff, well done! Secondly, it couldn't have been very successful because you voted for her anyway?'

'It wasn't really. It was difficult to second guess her; we didn't know if she'd play it straight or what so…'

'But you thought she might vote for me?' 'We did. You or Alex.'

'Really. Wow.'

Doc cuts short our conversation with an announcement to the room. 'We have the votes, to the unit we go! Leave your drinks.'

He sets off with a more relaxed walking pace this time. He's probably aware that the early buzz has worn off from the group. I wonder who Viola voted for?

Chapter Four
Single Figures.

It was a quiet walk to the unit. We were all close enough to hear each other talking so nobody did. The only thing of real interest was the complete shutdown of Desmond's limbs. Despite Hendon and Avon being close enough throughout the duration of the walk, he still managed to find a moment to try and charge off, only to veer headfirst into a wall. Hendon picked him up and carried him the rest of the way; he currently resides on the gurney, conscious but relatively incoherent, save for the odd swear word.

We have naturally circled around Doc, curious as to what he will say.

'Okay, the three groups have voted and come up with two names. The two names are Desmond and Viola. The remaining seven will each give me the name of the person they most suspect.

Four votes will decide it.'

I can't believe Viola managed to convince Agatha to vote for Desmond. Unless Amelia is lying to me, I don't think she would, I just can't believe Viola convinced Agatha to do it.

Meanwhile, if looks could kill, Viola would be surrounded by bodies. She's nailing the quiet rage. I quickly glance around at the others, trying to work out who will do what. This is gonna be close.

'Okay, let us begin,' Doc says, working things out on his clipboard, 'Clemence, who is your robot?'

I've noticed Clemence gravitating to the centre of the crowd, trying to blend in, anonymity, hoping the votes start from one end. Doc has apparently surveyed the clipboard and doesn't seem interested in the logistics. She looks mortified and Viola is staring daggers at her. 'Desmond.' she says.

'Okay,' he marks his paperwork, 'Kay?' The exact same thing happens. 'Desmond.' she says.

'Okay, two-nil. Amelia?' She thinks for a moment. 'Viola.' she says.

'Two-one, Avon?'

He rubs his scalp, pondering. 'Desmond.'

'Okay, three-one. Cliff?'

Oh dear. It's my go. After chatting in the dining room, she would assume that I would side with her. I can stand behind science and say that I voted for her because I didn't think Desmond could possibly be a machine. Alex will vote for her, if I do too it's three-three. It all comes down to Agatha. Maybe she went with Desmond under duress, she might not feel Viola's pressure as much in this crowd. This could be our chance to get her out.

'Viola.' I say.

'Three-two. Agatha?'

'Desmond.' she says, without consideration or contemplation. Wow.

'Okay, four-two. You've chosen Desmond.' Doc says,

looking quite surprised, almost shocked. I mean, Des can hardly walk, he's so drunk. He can't be a robot.

Hendon holds him in position on the gurney, while Alex F takes a sample. Desmond doesn't seem to notice, mumbling to himself and making the odd grunt.

We all wait patiently as the computer processes the sample, before again, revealing the expected result. I don't know how we keep getting this wrong, it's crazy.

'He's human,' Doc says, holding the results aloft. 'Hendon, please make sure he gets to his car safely.'

Hendon nods. He flips Desmond up off of the gurney and into a fireman's carry. They both disappear into the cold evening air and just like that, Desmond is gone. Doc has been whispering with Alex F and is ready to address the room.

'Nine becomes eight! Before we go on, there are a couple of things to say. Firstly, I think we can all agree that this evening's entertainment has been a total success! Creating a robot shell to house a complex computer system can be problematic but then to have the robot shell transformed into the image of a human being, so accurately that fellow peers can't tell which is which, it's just mind-boggling. Secondly, Alex will leave us now and retire to the fishbowl. I will take samples in her absence and to practise and to quieten thoughts, I will test her now.'

Alex F gives Doc a needle and rolls up her sleeve. He doesn't need practice, he takes the sample with immediacy and efficiency, planting it into the computer in one swift motion. After a beat, the result prints out. Again, he holds it aloft.

'Another human. Alex, will you say a few words before you leave?' Alex F visibly squirms and scrunches her nose.

'I would say that, if you haven't got lucky and guessed the robot by now, you probably won't. It will learn from the rest of you and veer the conversations towards suspecting others. I think it will be intelligent enough to stay one step ahead. Humans generally make two mistakes in this situation; you guys are making both. You think you're craftier than a robot and you're not, you can't accept that not only is it more intelligent, it's also more cunning. It learns from humans after all. The other thing you're doing is using your votes to settle personal vendettas, you're too busy squabbling as opposed to working together to solve a common problem. You just kicked Des out, a case in point. Was it because you thought he was a robot or because he was crass, drunk and disorderly? You chose to ignore the bigger problem and instead chose to solve your own selfish issues. It's very human. We've always done that as a race, and we always will. We can't help it.'

A strange parting shot and with that she leaves the room through the sliding door. I put my hand up, Doc notices.

'Cliff?'

'What's the fishbowl?'

'The fishbowl is a viewing gallery on the fourth floor. An observation deck if you will. I'm sure you've all noticed cameras sharing your space in here. They record back to the fishbowl so anyone in there can follow what's happening. Think of it as a security system of sorts. She normally goes up there, surveying events and eating carrots and hummus, getting grubby, greasy bits all over the keyboards.'

'Oh…will we go there?'

Doc is distracted, still reflecting on his own submission. 'Possibly.'

The rest of us look amongst ourselves, waiting for Doc to tell us what happens next. Suspicion grows.

'What now, Doc?' Avon asks.

Doc notices the prod and removes himself from his own thoughts. 'Right, well, we wait for Hendon to return!'

On cue, Hendon returns. He and Doc share a glance.

'Right, there's ten of us remaining in the room, the eight of you will be split into four groups of two and Hendon and I will take you to your own private areas. Each group will give me one name on their return to the medical unit. You will have thirty minutes to decide but I doubt any of you will need that long. Oh, and try to guess the robot this time. Alex was right, you seem to be choosing heart over head and we're running out of guests! Hendon, please escort Viola and Alex to the ground floor, second study please.'

Hendon nods but is obviously unsure if Doc will continue his piece first. Doc leaves him in no doubt.

'Are you waiting for a bus?' he asks sarcastically. Hendon grimaces and leads the two ladies away. 'Right, the rest of you, follow me!'

Doc leads the remaining group across the entrance hall and into the elevator. We see the others disappearing down a corridor. I wonder how that will go. I don't think Alex is a fan of Viola but she won't be able to vote for her, now they're together. Or vice versa.

The elevator stops on the second floor.

'Remember, ground floor when you're ready to come back. Kay and Amelia, follow me. The rest of you wait here.'

Doc presses the hold button and heads down the corridor. The two ladies follow. We all study them as Doc opens the last door on the left, says a few words to the two before heading back to us. He presses the hold button, releasing it from its job and we move up to the third.

I wonder who I'll be paired with? I've got to know the vibe of Avon and Clem; I don't really know Agatha at all.

The elevator doors slide open. The third floor is less cultured than the floors below, smaller too. There're only four doors along the walkway.

'Avon and Clemence, follow me.'

Doc does the same as before, even to the point of entering the last door on the left. A few words with those two and he's back in the lift, taking it to the fourth floor.

I suppose it's Agatha then. I won't run out of questions. I'll ask her why she voted for Desmond last time, I thought they were solid?

The doors swing open. The fourth floor is in worse shape than the third. Old wallpaper, cobwebs and damaged woodwork. It's like a haunted house. One door on either side of a short corridor. I think he said the fishbowl was on the fourth floor.

'Are we going to the fishbowl?' I ask.

'No!' he replies, frogmarching us to the door on the left.

'This is the fourth floor piano lounge.' Doc announces, opening the door and letting it swing open. Agatha and I peer in. It couldn't be further from the look of the approach.

A large and opulent area that wouldn't be out of place on a lower floor, complete with luxurious seating, an antique drinks cabinet, fully stocked of course and the clue is in the name: A grand piano. Floor to ceiling windows at the back of the room open onto a balcony that looks pristine and inviting. My breath is taken away and Agatha looks at me like she's just found a pot of gold. Doc is indifferent.

'Half an hour remember, ground floor.' he says before vanishing. We hear the elevator descending.

'Drink?' I say.

'Yes!' she says, 'I'll have what you're having!'

Agatha wanders the room, looking at the various trinkets and objet d'art.

I tackle the drinks cabinet, which is far too gentle for my coarse hands. I attempt a rum inspired cocktail with ice and lemon, though in this setting I should probably refer to it as being "on the rocks."

I walk the drinks across the room and out onto the balcony, where Agatha has positioned herself, admiring the view. I pass her the drink; she raises it to me before taking a sip. She doesn't pull a face so I assume it's passable. I take a swig and confirm it's passable. Just.

You can see for miles up here. It's dark but I can make out the countryside fields, trees, sheep, all the classics. Although we haven't spent much time together, Agatha and I have eased into a relaxed company. She's maybe several years younger than me, perhaps early thirties, attractive in a classic way. She seems comfortable in her own skin. If it is her own skin. I sit opposite her and we smile at each other, just enjoying the situation.

'It's weird, all this. Voting each other out. Doc is obviously…eccentric.' she says. 'That's one word for it.'

She laughs.

'Well, he's not a robot, he did the test!' she says. 'He did indeed.'

We fall silent. I decide to throw it out there. 'Can I ask you a question, Agatha?'

'Of course.' she responds.

'How come you voted for Desmond last time? I thought you two were hitting it off.'

Agatha shifts awkwardly in her seat, thinking through a response. Would a machine think through a response or have the answer ready to go? Could a robot already have the answer but play for time, acting the same way a human might? This game is becoming a headfuck.

'I'll be honest. When we arrived, I thought he was a good-looking boy. He came over and started giving me and Alex some spiel, I'm single so I didn't mind the flirtation. He said he wasn't drinking before he got here but he seemed overly confident, almost arrogant, I dunno, something was off.'

'Cocaine?' I suggest, half-joking.

'Maybe? Anyway, when we were in the bar earlier, with the pool tables?' I remember and nod.

'Well, he just seemed really drunk, he was getting a bit handsy and running down Teddy, you know, calling him nasty stuff. He laughed it off but it wasn't nice. Alex seemed to escape his attention so he focused on me. I was playing along but in truth, I was a bit scared. He was quite forceful and dictating, you know, making decisions for me, where I want to go, what I want to drink. We've only just met for Christ's sake, really controlling!'

'Sounds like a nightmare.' I say.

'Yeah. So I got put with Viola, she seemed a bit opinionated but as soon as I opened up about Desmond she was down with it. She said maybe you guys would vote for him as well so he'd be really in for it. When we got back to the dining room, he was up on the table, acting like a prick. When Hendon forced him down, he started being sick everywhere. It was embarrassing. I'm glad he's not here anymore.'

It's a pretty horrible story.

'I'm glad he's not here too.' I offer.

'Did you guys vote for him as well?' she says, fully expecting me to say yes.

Oh dear. If I lie, I'm worried it will come back to haunt me. It is tempting though. After hearing that story, how can I tell her that we decided to vote for the woman she confided in instead? This is a tricky spot. I think she's noticed that by how long it's taking me to form an answer, my response would be an unlikely truth. I think fast and open my mouth.

'I was with Alex and Kay and we made the decision together. It wouldn't be fair of me to disclose our choice. I am, however, completely satisfied that he was the one who went out.'

'I understand, very honourable.' she says, clearly impressed by my supposed virtue.

Phew. Got away with that. Maybe I'm the robot. Where did that come from? I take a large gulp of drink and change the subject. Well, sort of.

'So, we're on the clock, what's your impression of the others?'

Agatha strokes the bridge of her nose, carefully gathering her thoughts.

'Well, last time I was with Viola and Avon. Viola was quite keen on the game; I didn't get a robot vibe. Avon on the other hand, he's a bit quiet. Friendly but peripheral. Earlier, I was with

Desmond and Alex, Teddy also. I thought Alex was cool and the other two are out. Who else? I haven't talked to Kay much. I haven't talked to you much.'

She's thinking. I help out. 'Amelia and Clemence.'

'Oh yes, how could I forget Clemence! She's nice enough, a bit full on? I haven't had facetime with her so I'm not sure, she'd maybe get my vote if we were just picking…you know…' 'Annoying people?'

'Yeah!' she laughs.

'What about Amelia?' I ask, trying not to sound too interested. 'She's a strange one. We talked a bit during the pizza.'

'I thought you were tied up with Desmond?' I say, trying not to sound too defensive.

'I was but there were moments when he wasn't glued to my side!' she says, somewhat offended.

'Sorry.' I apologise. She's fine.

'Amelia was cool but she seemed a bit, I dunno, anti-establishment? Anarchic? She's playing the game though, following all the rules, so, her attitude didn't really play. I didn't ask her what she does for a job. I wonder if it alludes to the way she is or if it further explains the contradiction. You were with her on the beach weren't you? What did you find out?'

I'm not sure I like the way this conversation is going. I feel a bit defensive of Amelia. I don't know why.

'I didn't find out what her job was but we talked and I know what you mean, she's a bit alternative but I didn't get the feeling that she's a machine.'

Agatha rubs her nose again, she's suspicious. I'm not going to tell her that we felt each other's skin and it was incredibly intimate and there's no way she's a robot so I'm gonna tell her something else that hopefully allays her fears.

'We smoked a cigarette.' Agatha does a half smile.

'She had smokes on her and we sat in the woods, after the beach, and smoked. I didn't think she was a robot and that confirmed it for me.'

'You might be lying. Trying to trick me into thinking you're not the robot. And even if you did both smoke, everyone here eats and drinks and spits. Maybe the robot can smoke. It might not prove anything.' she says calmly.

'You're not drinking?' I say, gesturing towards the cocktail that I gave her, the same one she hasn't gone back to since.

She picks up the glass and takes a few gulps. 'Okay?' she says, smiling.

'Okay.' I say, smiling back.

There's no animosity between us, more of a friendly distrust. I suppose this game brings that out in all of us.

'So what about you? You don't think it's Amelia, who else have you gauged?' I think about the rest of the horde.

'I was with Alex and Kay last time; I don't suspect either. I hung out with Amelia, I've talked with Clemence, again, I don't suspect either.'

'What about me?' she asks.

'Well,' I stumble, 'we can't vote for each other anyway so it's moot.' Agatha acknowledges.

'I can't vote for myself so I guess right now it would be Avon or Viola.' I say.

'Okay, well after listening to your inconclusive assessment I would throw Kay and Clemence in, I don't know Kay yet but there's something I'm not sure about and as for Clemence, she is annoying, maybe it's intentional, hidden in plain sight?'

'Maybe you're making it more complicated than it is?'
'Maybe. I just think she's a bit…you know.'

'Yeah, I know.' I say.

'Well let's get to it then. I'll save one of yours, you save one of mine and we'll decide between the other two together. I'll save Viola. She's intense but I don't think it's her. You go. Save Kay or Clem?'

I'm not happy but it seems fair at least. 'I'll save Kay.' I say.

'Okay. It's Avon or Clemence. I do think Avon is odd but I'm not sure if he's the machine. Clem might be the machine, she talks about herself incessantly, maybe it's a ruse to make the rest of us think she's a putz; to come across like that so we would never suspect her. I'm sticking with Clem, thoughts?'

I sigh loudly.

'Okay, I'm not mad about it but I understand what you're saying. Let's vote for Clem.' 'We've reached an agreement.' she says, raising her glass to me and smiling.

I nod back and give my drink another go.

The elevator ride down was uneventful, the entrance hall is so much more luxurious than the corridor we experienced on the fourth floor. I watch Agatha closely, her walk and the way she turns her head. I wonder if any of the other guests suspect her? After spending time with her, she's landed on my radar. I'm noticing everything, every time she flicks her hair or scratches her elbow, I judge whether it's human or some form of anthropoid, trying to achieve a natural form. Inside the medical unit, we are the last to arrive. There are guilty looks on many faces. Doc rushes us back to the sliding door.

'You've made a decision?' he says quietly.

'Yes.' I say. He stands so close I can smell his stale breath. Agatha moves slowly into the room, leaving me to do the dirty work.

'And?'

'Clemence.' I whisper.

'Thank you.' he says, scribbling on his pad.

He waves me into the others and stands in front of us all.

'I have the votes and I can say there are four different nominations.' Interesting.

'I will now read the names of the four nominations. If your name isn't called, follow me to the entrance hall. Clemence. Cliff. Kay. Viola. I'll be back shortly. Everyone else, follow me!'

Doc exits the room, the other four, sheepishly and quickly filter out. The remainder look at each other with a mixture of surprise and acceptance. Viola is trying to conceal her anger and talks through gritted teeth.

'All of our groups voted for different people and you can't choose yourself.' she says, looking us up and down.

'Having gotten to know you this evening, I'm gonna take an educated guess as to who picked who. Avon has got a thing about Cliff and persuaded Clemence to vote that way. Equally, Agatha has a thing for Clemence and persuaded Cliff to do the same. That would suggest that Kay and Amelia voted for me.'

Viola stands in front of Kay menacingly, eye to eye.

'By that assumption, it means that you voted for me as well.' Kay says.

'Maybe we did. Me and Alex were the first ones back here, so we'd know who got paired together. You and Amelia weren't here much long after so you must have come to your decision pretty quickly?' Viola doesn't blink.

Kay isn't comfortable but isn't backing down. I decide to jump in. 'Why has Avon got a thing for me?'

'You were the last one to arrive, he can't get past it, I mean it did seem odd, you know, that you were late.' Clem says.

'Maybe I was just late, there was traffic, it was completely innocent!' I try. 'I don't know what to tell you, he won't let go of it.'

Clemence and I stare at each other, accepting the decision. 'Why did you vote for me?' she asks quietly.

'Agatha argued that maybe you talk about yourself a lot because you've been programmed that way so that nobody suspects you, they just think you're…'

Her eyes widen, I don't know what to say. Viola helps. 'Self-centred?'

Ouch. Clem is visibly wounded. 'I see.' she says solemnly.

Silence takes the room, momentarily, until Viola takes it back.

'So, that seems like confirmation. They voted for each other, which means we voted for each other Kay. Spill it, why did you vote for me?'

Clearly, Kay is not happy with the direct approach that Viola is taking. 'It's just a game Vi, we have to choose someone?' she says.

'I know it's just a game, why me though?'

Kay looks around the room, unsure of what to say. Viola stares intently at her with an insistence. Even Clem and I are watching with bated breath. You could cut the atmosphere with a knife. 'We chose you because Amelia said you have a propensity to plant the idea of someone being the machine into other people's heads, thus turning the attention away from you. It's the kind of thing that the robot would do.' she says without looking Viola in the eye.

'Didn't you defend me? I thought we were friends Kay?'

'We are friends! I didn't know who to vote for and Amelia made a fair point and anyway, it's only a game! Besides, you chose me so we're in the same boat!'

It's quite the outburst. Kay meets eyes and looks defiant, confident almost. A faint smirk crosses Viola's face. Clem and I watch on, this is turning ugly.

The sliding door parts, and Doc returns to the centre of the room, the four others mooch in behind, relieving the tension. Or exchanging the tension. Here we go again. Doc waits for complete silence before relaying.

'The four have chosen to save two of you, two votes each in fact, so the two that have been saved will follow me to the entrance hall to make the final call. Viola, Cliff, it's you. Let's go.'

He exits and Viola and I follow. Hendon approaches the door and stands on the threshold, arms crossed. We go to the centre of the hall with Doc.

'Okay, you two will choose the robot now, Clemence or Kay.' he says, standing with us, as if part of the group.

'Are you gonna stand there?' I say politely to him. 'I am.' he says.

'Well, what are you thinking?' Viola says, unconcerned with his presence. 'I don't know, I don't really suspect either.'

'It's no time for altruism Cliff, you have to pick one. I like them both but my hand is forced, I'll pick Kay.'

Doc smiles, he's loving it.

'Is that because she just stood up to you?' I ask.

'No, of course not. Clemence is more real. Kay is quite reserved and straddling the fence all the time. It's an actual stab at guessing the machine.'

Viola looks emotionless, maybe she's the robot. I mull over what she's saying and I agree totally. I've not considered Kay but she is blending into the background. Perhaps it makes her more ambiguous. Doc is enjoying my struggle, beaming at me without a shred of decency. I can smell his breath again. He hovers, but in my personal space. It's unsettling.

'Okay,' I say, 'Let's vote for Kay.'

Viola nods, Doc rubs his hands together and the three of us enter the medical unit once more. Hendon slides the door shut and Doc takes his place next to the gurney, readying a needle and making sure his clipboard is in touching distance.

'Everyone, a decision has been made. Kay, you have been voted most likely. Please, come to the gurney.'

Kay gives a wry smile, shaking her head with a look of disgust and rolling her sleeve up. Doc administers the needle and swiftly puts the findings into the machine. We watch silently as he removes the results and studies the screen, eventually turning to face us.

'You've done it again. Another human. Hendon, please escort Kay to her driver. Have you anything to say before you leave us?'

Kay thinks for a moment before looking at Doc.

'Thank you for this evening, it's been fun.' she says, before turning to Viola, 'It's nice to meet you all, well, most of you, good luck.'

Hendon and Kay leave the room and the dust settles.

'The magnificent seven!' Doc proclaims, to no reaction whatsoever, 'Follow me to the elevator!' He races from the room, excited and vigorous. He reminds me of Willy Wonka.

The rest of us follow and squeeze into the elevator. There's more room in it than earlier but it's still close. I'm staring at the back of Viola's head as we make our way upwards. The doors open and Doc heads out and right. Following him reveals that we are in the pub area from earlier, with all the spitting. He leads us over to the bar and holds his finger out, as if pausing for something. From close by, we can all hear grunting and clattering, it sounds like a pig in a war. Hendon appears behind the bar, sweaty and red. He must have raced up behind us on the stairs. Doc looks at him scornfully.

'Can you make a selection of drinks please Hendon, if it's not too much to ask?'

Hendon picks up on the patronising tone and starts busying himself with trays and glasses. Doc shakes his head, really laying on the theatrics for the rest of us. Eventually, he checks his clipboard and addresses us.

'You've collectively chosen six human beings over the robot so far. Now, I'm sure you've all read or heard about the advancements in artificial intelligence over the last several years but it's always seemed a distant thought, mainly because it lives inside of computers or servers.

However, the future is now, we have created the prosthetics to successfully harbour a replicant that walks among us. Undetected, so far, the replicant is learning from you, all the time, which will make it even more difficult to distinguish. There are seven of you left, six if you think about it. Relax in the bar, discuss the situation, when you have decided who you think is the machine, come to the medical unit and cast your vote. This is not a group round; you will vote individually and draw your own conclusions. I will be waiting there and until then, Hendon will attempt to meet your requirements. I wish you luck.'

He casts quite a sombre mood and walks from the room in a casual manner, very unlike him. Not like Willy Wonka at all.

Hendon places a tray of various drinks on the bar. Avon shuffles to the toilet. 'It's awkward because we're all in here.' Amelia says to me.

'Yes.' I agree.

The other ladies collect drinks and start to sit around a large table next to the serving area, chattering quietly. Amelia and I are left at the bar. She takes what looks like a gin and tonic from the tray and enjoys a deep swig from it.

'That's gin.' she confirms happily.

I pick up what must be a Guinness and take a gulp to confirm my suspicions. 'Vodka?' She toys.

'Yep,' I say, 'I could tell by the colour.'

She takes out her cigarettes. Hendon watches from across the bar. 'Can I smoke in here?' she asks him.

Hendon looks put out, thinking carefully before reaching under the bar and bringing out a classic, bronze ashtray. He sits it in front of her.

'Thanks Hendon.' she says, with surprise.

She takes one out and lights it, offers me one, which I decline and so she puts the pack away. 'You don't fancy one?'

'No, I'm getting that headache, you know, when you drink a few pints and slow down. If I stop drinking before I get slaughtered, I always get a sort of headache.'

She takes the smokes back out and plonks one in front of me. 'Well don't stop then.' she says.

Fair enough. She passes me a lighter and I do the routine and pass it back. She nods at me to look at the table behind us. I see Alex and Agatha leaving their seats and sitting down together on another table next to the far wall, leaving Clem and Viola alone. Viola notices us watching. 'We thought it better to split up, so we can all put our thoughts across easier.' she says, throwing Amelia a filthy look before returning her gaze to Clem.

'She's got it in for you,' I say to Amelia, 'she worked out that you and Kay voted for her.' 'Good, we did. She's a witch.'

'Do you think she'll vote for you this time?'

'Probably. I don't care, I'm gonna vote for her. She's a witch.'

'Maybe she'll try and persuade Clem and the others to vote for you as well though, you'll be knackered.' I say with concern.

'I'm not sure she could convince the others. With the exception of Clem, she's running out of allies. Besides, I've heard rumours about someone else that might carry weight.'

She looks at me and raises her eyebrows for effect, drinking her gin but not leaving my gaze. I'm swept up in curiosity. I guess that was the intention.

Avon returns from the loo and sidles up next to us, potentially ruining the chance of a possible revelation.

'Blimey, more alcohol.' he says, exhausted by the excess. 'You getting a headache Avon?' Amelia says.

He holds his head, testing it out it seems. 'A little.'

'Well my advice is to keep on drinking. Cliff'll look after you. Right boys, I'm gonna hang around the girl chat, get the goss, I'll be back.'

Amelia grins and strolls over to where Alex and Agatha are sitting. She puts her drink down and slides into a seat. Avon and I share a difficult moment, I swig from my drink, and he chooses one from the tray. It looks like a pint of lager.

'Here we are then.' I say. He sort of smiles at me.

Chapter Five
An Unexpected Alliance.

'What are you thinking then, Cliff? We're the only boys left.' he says, sipping his pint and carefully setting it down on a mat.

'I know, it's not looking like they made a machine in the image of a man, is it?' 'Maybe not,' he laughs, 'have you got any likely suspects?'

'Not really. The truth is, whenever someone gets eliminated, we get back into the game, like now, and I haven't got anyone in mind. I really don't know.'

'How do you choose then?' he asks.

'I guess I'm usually influenced by someone else's opinions or discoveries. What about you?' 'Well, first of all, I don't really worry about this game too much. I'm surprised I haven't been kicked out yet. I question whether any of us are a robot or whether the Krelboyne Institute has been wasting all of our money on places like this. Cleaners, gardeners and all of the affluence. I mean, I haven't seen hints of laboratories or obvious workspaces. Other than the makeshift unit we keep going to. It's very strange. That said, I have been people watching and ascertaining certain information from our peers.'

'Like what?' I say, 'Do you know who you're going to vote for already?' 'I wouldn't go that far.'

'Is that why you keep voting for me?' I say, jokingly. He smiles.

'I haven't voted for you every time, you turned up late and I can't seem to get past it, so, if in doubt…'

'Vote for Cliff?' I say. We're both laughing now. It's jovial. But also true.

'Being practical, I don't know why they would make an older looking robot. Clem and I are the oldest people here I think, followed by Viola and then maybe you?' he says.

'Maybe,' I say, 'I'm just not convinced that age would factor into it.' He scratches his chin, reluctantly agreeing.

'I won't vote for you this time. What say we vote the same way? Stick together from here on out, make a pact?' he says.

I think.

'Okay. But who?'

Avon looks across the room, considering the others before turning back to me.

'There's five of them. We'll take turns to keep one safe until there's one left. We'll both vote for that one. Fair?'

'Fair.' I say. It is fair, I guess. I'd like to hear what Amelia has to say though, she was on the verge of telling me something influential. Possibly.

'Okay. You go first. Pick one to make safe.'

I look across the room. Alex and Agatha are sat on a distant table, deep in discussion. Amelia sits at the closer table now, with Clem and Viola.

Obviously, I like Amelia, I've a soft spot for her. A soft spot could be considered the inbred, half-nephew of a blind spot though. I don't want Avon thinking I'm sweet on her. He seems to have thought about the age card and probably thinks Clemence is clean. I think she is too.

Annoying but clean. I'll safe bet on her this time and if he doesn't pick her, Amelia next time. Play it cool.

'Clemence.' I announce quietly.

It's Avons turn to consider the options. He strokes his eyebrows, deep in contemplation. If he thinks about age, he'll save Viola. If he was thinking that though, he would've called quickly. He's thinking too long. For someone who isn't bothered by the game, he's really struggling. Finally, he turns to me and leans in.

'Alex,' he says, 'your go.'

I look across the room, trying to imitate someone who is internally debating and agonising over a decision, when in reality, I'm definitely saving Amelia. I drag it out for nearly a minute, trying to assure Avon that my answer is strictly business.

'Amelia.' I say.

'I knew you'd pick her; you like her Clifford!' he says, pushing on my shoulder playfully. I imagine I go red and coy.

'Your go.' I say, smiling. It's a fair cop.

We both settle down and drink, facing away from the others. There's no need to look. It's Agatha or Viola.

'What a dilemma.'

He's clearly having a tough time with this one. I must say, I don't envy him. Viola can be forceful, obnoxious even, but a machine? I'm not sure about that. On the other hand, Agatha seems friendly, amenable. I was with her last time and her behaviour raised a few doubts for me though. Do we vote for who we think is the robot or do we vote for, well, do we vote for Viola?

What if it is Viola? Oh dear. I'm glad it's not me deciding. Amelia waltzes to the bar and sits on the other side of me. Both Avon and I smile at her, somewhat pleased by the interruption.

Hendon appears before her.

'Gin and Tonic, on the rocks, with a dash of lime and have you got any of them little umbrellas that I can stir it with?' she asks.

'No.'

'What a shame.'

Hendon busies himself with the order. Amelia turns to us.

'You will not believe the information I have.' she says, through pursed lips.

Avon and I lean towards her, both curious and wide eyed. She looks at the optics, pretending not to notice us, cool as a cucumber.

'Well, are you gonna spill it?' I say, as quietly as possible.
'Patience men, let me get my drink.'

Avon laughs and goes back to his own drink; I do the same. All of us, watching Hendon go through the motions. He's quite adept at the craft but not quick enough for my liking. I'm itching to find out the news, plus, Avon is apparently choosing who we both vote for. I agreed to it, after all.

Hendon puts the finishing touches to the drink and finally presents it.

'Thanks Hendon.' she says, gazing at the glass, instead of downing it and sharing the bloody news.

Amelia takes what seems like an eternity to take a swig and drag out the anticipation, it's painful. Then she takes out another cigarette and lights it, Hendon quickly finds the ashtray he cleaned and places it accurately beneath her arm. She smiles at him. He grunts and walks off. She turns to us.

'Okay, quiet voices. I know who they're voting for.' 'Who's they?' I say.

'All of them. I know who they're all gonna vote for.' 'How.' Avon says.

'They told me.' My god.

'Are you gonna tell us then or carry on with this ridiculous charade?' I say, nicely but obviously perplexed.

'Calm down Cliff, wow.' she says, looking around to make sure nobody can hear. Amelia leans in even closer, Avon and I do the same. We're now huddled at the bar. An onlooker would say we looked very suspicious. Amelia spills.

'Viola and Clemence are voting for Agatha, Agatha and Alex are voting for Viola. The three of us can decide between those two and ultimately, get that person out.'

'Why are those two voting for Agatha?' Avon asks.

'Well, that's the other thing. Viola won't name names but she says she has it on good authority that Agatha doesn't sweat. When she was at the beach earlier, the air conditioning there was warmer and we all spent time there. Some people noticed that she wasn't sweating. I mean, Des took his top off, it was warm and it's unusual if she didn't get hot and bothered.'

'Who noticed?' I say. I didn't notice. 'She won't name names.'

'Alex was with her, she must've mentioned it.' Avon says.

'Maybe, but those two are sitting over there, getting on just fine. Maybe someone else noticed when they were in the beach area. Did either of you notice?' Amelia asks.

I shake my head.

'I didn't go to the beach.' Avon offers. 'Well Viola is dead set on it.' she says.

'Why are the other two voting for Viola?' I say.

Amelia looks at me, giving the impression that I've asked a rhetorical question. 'Because she's a tosser.'

Avon lets out a short, sharp guffaw which draws the attention of everyone. I look apologetic. Amelia drinks her drink.

'So, who are you guys voting for? I assume you've been over here, plotting and scheming?' she says.

I look to Avon, unsure as to what we should say, we made a pact, after all.

'Well,' he says, 'first of all, we discussed the validity of the game, is there even a robot among us or is it a distraction, so that we won't be as horrified when we find out that they've spent all of our money on this wildly elaborate paradise.'

'Okay…' she says.

'Then we turned our attention to the job at hand, talked about you ladies and whittled it down to two. Cliff, tell her.'

I focus on Amelia's crystal blue eyes. 'Agatha or Viola.' I say.

She smirks.

'Well, well. Interesting…And?'

'We're yet to decide.' he says, arousing mystery. 'Who are you voting for?' I ask Amelia.

'I'm gonna vote for Viola, obvs. Also, if you two vote for me, I'll have two votes, so that way, I'll guarantee my safety,

Viola will have three votes, guaranteeing her, disappearing from my mind. It's a win win. Not that you will vote for me, I'm just saying.'

She downs the rest of her drink.

'Now, I'm going down there to vote for Vi, I wonder if Doc has got something exciting happening for the people who go and vote. With what we've seen so far, I can't imagine I'm just gonna be sitting on the gurney, waiting for everyone else?'

''Maybe you will though. Are you sure about being down there with him, alone?' I say.

'Ha, I'm sure I'll be alright, I'm certainly drunk enough!' she says, loud enough to draw attention. With that, she stands up from the barstool, salutes, holds her hand in place for everyone to appreciate it and meanders through the bar to the elevator. She still has a cigarette on the go. Hendon isn't sure whether to intercept her or stay at the bar, attending to everyone else. He's frozen with indecision. She's gone.

I turn to Avon and raise my eyebrows. He returns the gesture and we both spin back to our drinks. The others noticed her exiting so I imagine we're all having similar conversations. Avon speaks quietly.

'If what she said is right, it's Viola, three and Agatha, two. Our votes will be essential to the verdict.'

'Yeah,' I reply, 'and it's your go.'

'And you'll go with my decision, regardless?' 'I will, we made a pact.' I say.

'We're here to find the robot, so I'm tempted to go for Agatha, however, we're also here to have a pleasant evening and I find her easier to relate to than Viola.' he says, deep in contemplation. Avon spins his chair back to the room and scans across it.

'Heads up.' he whispers to me.

I turn my head, following his gaze. It appears Clemence is also exiting the room.

Viola sits alone now, studying her drink and looking somewhat fragile. Normally fierce and confrontational, she sits still, with a vulnerability in her eyes. I guess she doesn't know she's being watched.

'Agatha.' Avon whispers to me, still watching Viola.

I nod the affirmative while struggling to hide a startled expression. I didn't think he'd say that but we made a pact.

Viola visibly pulls herself together and looks at Agatha and Alex, debating whether to approach. She sighs and looks towards us. We quickly look around towards Hendon and nervously glance at each other, like schoolboys who think they have just gotten away with one.

'Hi guys.' Viola says, sitting on the stool next to Avon.

We both greet her with a smile. She places her drink on the bar.

'It's starting to get pretty deceitful now. Loads of talking behind each other's backs. The whispering walls. What are you two thinking?' she says.

'Well, we've been discussing whether or not there's actually a robot among us?' Avon says.

'I know, it's tough to believe but these days, you only have to look into A.I for five minutes and you'll see something you didn't think possible. Not just the idea of it but that it already exists. 2005 was the last time a human beat a robot at chess. I don't know if either of you play chess but it's an extremely complex game, and 2005 was twenty odd years ago. Now think of all the other things that robots have been trained to do since, as well as the fact that they're self-learning. Now imagine all this data combined and placed together, inside a realistic humanoid. You would think it would be impossible to distinguish. There's been conversations, moments ago, about someone who doesn't sweat but I mean, there's drinking and smoking, so I don't know if that's a determining characteristic or...'

'What have you heard?' Avon says innocently.

He's playing the game. He said he wasn't really worried about it but, he's playing. 'Well, a few people have mentioned Agatha, on the beach.'

'Who?' I say.

'Well, I don't want to say, but...we were all there.'

'Avon wasn't there? I was there but didn't notice? Did you notice?'

'I mean,' she struggles, 'not noticed but in retrospect, I remember it being hot there. One of the lads took his top off.'

'But did you notice?' I probe.

Viola isn't keen on direct questioning; she may lash out.

'No but other people did and that's good enough for me!' she says, loud enough for Alex and Agatha to look over.

'So, are you gonna vote for her?' Avon asks in lowered tones.

Viola composes herself.

'Yes and you should too. According to Amelia, Agatha's voting for you and she's probably convincing Alex to do the same. One more Hendon.'

Viola finishes her drink and waves the empty glass in the air. Hendon takes it and starts doing the honours.

'Right. I'm gonna go and vote for her then.' Avon says, standing.

He makes sure Viola isn't watching before throwing me an odd look, followed by a raised eyebrow, confirming we will vote the same way. I give another affirmative nod back and he disappears.

I suppose the odd look was explained by the fact that Amelia told us that those two were voting for Viola and then Viola told us that they were voting for Avon. Maybe Viola said that to shore up more votes for Agatha and keep herself off the hook. Finding the robot has become secondary to winning by any means necessary. Very human.

Hendon places a new drink in front of Viola, who has a good crack at it before turning to me.

'I need to find this robot, Cliff,' she says, sounding a bit pissed, 'I haven't had much luck lately in life, I'm overdue a win. I know people here probably think I'm a bit much but I just wanna win one. Do you think I'm a bit much?'

Oof. I should have left instead of Avon.

'No…no, we're all different, aren't we?'. I manage, 'some people are more…forward than others.'

She's not buying it.

'I just think you guys don't care about it as much as me. You all just wanna have a good time, do you just wanna have a good time?'

I do, generally, want to have a good time.

'Yes?' I say. It's more of a question than a statement. Viola grimaces.

'Do you think it's me? Do you think I'm a robot?' she says, pointing at her chest. 'No, I don't.' I say confidently, before stupidly adding, 'it's one of us though.' She eyes me up and down, sobering up rapidly, which is strange.

'Maybe it's you, Cliff. Doing the backseat driver routine.

Making sure you do enough to stay in everybody's good books but little enough to avoid suspicion. I'm watching you.'

She sits back in her stool and stares at me, featureless. I feel very uncomfortable. I feel like I should tell her a secret, even though she's probably the most unlikable person here. I want to feel sorry for her, but she's so mean. I stand.

'I'm going to go and vote now, I'm not going to vote for you.' I say, earnestly.

She inspects me without changing her expression. I leave my drink on the bar and after a moment of waiting to see if Viola would say anything, I turn and leave. Alex and Agatha watch me depart but there's no acknowledgement.

I feel flustered as I wait for the elevator, tapping the button repeatedly, irritated by it not being there, open for business. I decide to take the stairs as the lift doors open, catching me off balance as I'd shifted my weight to advance to the stairwell. I enter and the doors slide shut. 'Ground floor.' I say aloud.

The elevator begins descending. I try to gather my thoughts. I felt hot under the collar in the bar but for the first time since I arrived, a cold shiver runs through me. The exchange with Viola really moved me. I'm just not sure in which direction.

The doors open and spew me into the lobby. Across the way, Doc stands at the unit entrance, rubbing his hands with glee and bobbing about. I make my way over to him.

'Here comes one!' he calls into the room, leaving out who it is on purpose, trying to build the excitement.

'Who are you voting for, Cliff?' Doc quietly asks as I meet him at the threshold.

I think quickly, I made a pact with Avon and despite leaning towards Viola, though it's mainly because she's nasty, I'm sticking to it. For now. I hope he does.

'Agatha.' I respond.

'In you go then!' he says, stepping aside.

I enter the medical unit and see Amelia, Clemence and Avon, standing together in the middle of the room.

'Alright.' I say.

'Not really,' Amelia replies, 'there's no chairs, there's nothing to do, Doc keeps suggesting we play "I Spy", which is starting to grate and the others might be up in the bar for ages, I wish I'd never come down!'

'First world problems!' Doc calls, eavesdropping from the door. 'Piss off!' Amelia returns.

Doc smiles inanely. Water off a duck's back.

I sit on the gurney, surprised that none of them have done it, when I feel a sharp pain in my lower back and jump up, clutching my kidney. Doc stands behind me, holding what looks like a taser or stun gun. He fires it so I can see a blue, electrical current running between its sensors. 'No sitting on the bed, old boy.'

'Understood.' I won't need telling again.

Doc stands back at the entrance, I waddle to the group, still rubbing my side.

'He did that to Clemence when she arrived,' says Amelia, shaking her head, 'what a piece of work.'

'Why didn't you tell me that before I sat down!?' I ask, showing as much restraint as I can. 'We thought it'd be funny.' Amelia says, deadpan.

I smile. It's funny. My side hurts, it's quite a powerful bit of kit, but that was a funny response. 'Are you alright?'

Clemence asks me.

'Not really.' I reply.

'So what's going on up there?' Avon asks, 'sorry for leaving you with Viola.'

'Yeah, you did scarper a bit sharpish,' I smile, 'she was just doing the go to sob story mixed with naked aggression and sinister threat. You know what she's like.'

Amelia enjoys my throwaway style and laughs heartily. Even Avon chuckles. 'Is she worried about being voted for?' Clem asks.

'Yes but no more than every other exchange we've had.' I reply. 'She should be worried,' Amelia grunts, 'she's a witch.'

'What are the other three doing up there?' Avon asks.

'Alex and Agatha were still sitting together on that far table, Viola was sitting at the bar, alone with her thoughts.'

'Crikey. By the way, I asked Doc about the whole "Is there actually a robot here or is this just an elaborate way of getting rid of us?" and he assured me that there is. He's going to make a call after this round, providing we don't guess correctly, to see if they can prove it to us, before going any further.' Avon says to me.

'Well either way, I'm having fun.' Amelia interjects.

'I'm not sure if this would be a ruse, I mean, wouldn't we have something to say about where all of our money has gone?' Clem states.

'Not if they're kicking us out one by one, there won't be anyone left here to complain. I want proof.' Avon replies.

'Here comes one!' Doc exclaims, looking across the hall, out of our view. 'Who is it?' Clem asks.

'You'll see…' Doc says, sloping towards the person, out of view. 'I bet it's her.' Amelia snarls, meaning Viola I assume.

The room falls silent. Each of us anticipating the conversations that are about to unfold. I hope it isn't Viola but given the lay of the land up there, a betting man would put his money on it. We can hear murmurs from the hallway but nothing that alludes to the guest in question. We look amongst ourselves with quizzical expressions. No one knows.

'They're out there for a long time?' Clem says.

'There must be something else to discuss?' Avon says.

Another moment passes. Footsteps approach the door, here we go. It's Alex. She nods a greeting and walks over to us. Doc assumes his role as bouncer.

'There's no chairs?'

'No,' Clem says, 'and don't sit on the bed, he'll zap you.' 'You tell her but not me?' I say half-heartedly.

Alex looks confused. Avon jumps in. 'What's going on up there?'

Alex grins.

'Well, after Cliff left, Viola came over and started casting aspersions. Agatha took exception to some of the remarks and the situation escalated. I was getting between them but they were calling each other names and pointing fingers, it turned really bad. Hendon got between them in the end, poor bloke, he told me to come here and wait and that he'd calm the other two down and get them here.'

'Blimey,' Avon replies, 'what were they arguing about?'

'Viola was implying that earlier on, Agatha told her something in confidence, she didn't say what it was, but it was a lie. She had found out something that suggested

Agatha had lied and challenged her. Agatha said that it proved that Viola had a big mouth because word had gotten back to her, meaning Viola had told someone else and hadn't kept it to herself. Then it turned into a slanging match. They both stood up and started pushing each other, threatening violence. I went between them and tried to separate them but they were both too strong to keep apart.

Luckily, Hendon came over and physically removed me from the situation and told me to leave.' All of us are gobsmacked.

'Did you vote?' asks Amelia. 'Yes.' Alex replies.

'Viola is trouble. She's been pulling the strings for too long. She's gotta go. She probably is a robot, getting us to vote for each other and turning us against each other, she's a witch.' Amelia says.

'Well, we've already voted so we'll see.' Avon responds.

'Well I can't see why any of you would have voted for someone else?' Amelia begins, 'She's overtly horrible. Her idea of friendship is to turn someone into a gopher who will do her bidding and run around, meeting her needs, it's not reciprocal. She's arrogant, but in fairness to her, she doesn't put on a face, she's openly arrogant. She's a tosser.'

'Not a witch?' I joke.

Amelia doesn't acknowledge.

'She's a nasty piece of work, she's quite rude, she's affecting the atmosphere this evening and she's gotta go.'

A short silence falls over the statement before Doc, who is clearly enthralled by the debate, speaks.

'Here they are, you lot stay here.'

He removes himself from sight. The rest of us wait. Are we going to see black eyes or fat lips? How far did it go? This is going to be tense. Murmurs from the hallway grow closer, as do footsteps.

Viola enters the room and flashes a smile, taking her place next to me. Agatha follows, looking angry and staring at the floor. She stands at the other end of the group, next to Alex. Neither have cuts or bruises, well, none that I can see. Doc stands next to the gurney; Hendon mans the door.

'So, I have the votes.' Doc says.

He waits, looking around, trying to build anticipation. It's working.

'Four of you received zero votes, two of you received two votes each and one of you received three votes. We have a decision.'

Again he pauses, giving me time to wonder why this has happened because according to my maths in the bar, Agatha would get four votes and Viola would get three. Now I don't know who voted for who and certain people said one thing and did another.

'Agatha, I'm afraid it is you who has been chosen. Please approach.'

Agatha advances, sullen. As Doc administers the needle and goes through the rigmarole, I work out in my head that Agatha got the three, presumably Viola got two votes and who else got two votes? And who voted for them? I study the rest of the group, they look as suspicious as I do, perhaps having worked out the maths themselves.

'Human.' Doc announces, 'Anything to say, Agatha dear?'

'It's not Viola but vote her out anyway, she should be ashamed.' she says. Agatha walks to the exit door.

'See her out please Hendon. Then make drinks in the biodome.' Doc says. Hendon nods and shepherds Agatha out.

'Then there were six!' Doc says, loudly and proudly.

'What about this proof?' Avon asks, trying to take the wind from his sails.

'Ah yes. The proof. Follow me to the biodome and all will be revealed, come!' Doc quickly gathers a few items from the desk and gallops off.

The six of us pile after him with less enthusiasm. Knowing that the biodome is on the ground floor and not terribly far away, I expect everyone is comfortable making it there in their own sweet time.

Part of me half expected Agatha to be the replicant. She had an unusual way about her. I study the other five, no closer to determining the culprit. Maybe it is me. I do think Avon has a point in saying he'd like proof. However, if Doc can prove that there's a robot among us, the game is gonna get serious. Or more serious.

We reach the biodome and gather inside the entrance. Doc stands next to the drinks table, on a mobile phone. His other hand is covering his mouth so it's impossible to determine who he's talking to or what is being said. No sign of Hendon, God help him.

'Okay.' Doc says, hanging up the phone and pocketing it. 'We have a plan. We will prove that there is a robot in our midst.'

Hendon scuttles to the table with a massive tray of drinks, each of them different but all have liquid sloshing about. No spillages though as he switches the empty tray out. Doc isn't appreciating the dexterity.

'Go and fetch a beach towel, Hendon,' he says. Hendon looks at him, unsure of the request. Doc sighs.

'Put the tray on the floor, forget about it. Go and fetch a

beach towel, now please.'

Hendon follows his orders, Doc shakes his head, removes the items from his pockets and starts to undress. I don't know what this proof will entail but if getting naked and fetching a beach towel are involved, I'd rather not know.

We all watch, bewildered, as he removes his three-quarter length surgical gown and his jumper. He notices all eyes on him.

'Calm down everyone, I won't go all the way, not yet anyway!' he laughs, unbuttoning and removing his shirt.

Thankfully, it appears that that's the end of it, leaving a vest on the top half, covering his modesty. He takes the items off of the floor and walks into a return, next to the entrance. 'Now here, I have six test tubes in a rack, six needles and some gauze.'

He shows us the items, bringing them up off the ground and placing them back.

'I've taken my clothes away so you can see I have nothing up my sleeves with which to tamper the results. I will conduct this exercise in the corner here, so you can see no means of outside interference. Avon, as you have been vocal about proof, will you come and check over the instruments to ensure that everything meets your approval, please?'

Avon walks over to the corner, picking up the medical paraphernalia and examining the wall, as if it's a crime scene, or some kind of magic illusion.

Satisfied, Avon returns to the audience. Hendon appears and unfurls a rather small looking towel.

'I said a towel, not a flannel!'

Doc smiles, hoping that his joke landed. It did not.

'Well, that will have to do. Stand where I'm standing, holding the towel out as you have it.'

Doc moves to one side, allowing Hendon to do just that. He then stands behind Hendon, who is a large man and obscures the view of Doc, almost entirely.

'Now, Avon, if you approach Hendon, stand on the other side of the towel and roll up your sleeve.'

Doc is raising his voice because we can't see his face, it's bizarre. Avon does as he was asked.

'Now, put your arm around the towel and look away. I will take a sample and transfer it to a test tube. I will do this with each of you, okay?'

Nobody speaks but Avon does as he was told and Doc begins.

Throughout the ordeal, Doc balances the test tube rack behind the towel, as well as administering the injections with a new needle every time. Sometimes holding a used one in his mouth, horizontally of course, it's a deft balancing act and somewhat unprofessional.

After Avon, Viola, Alex, Amelia, Clemence and I go through the "plan", Doc speaks.

'I will mix up the order of the six test tubes so you won't know whose is whose, bring the towel down to the floor Hendon, slowly!' he shouts, worrying that Hendon will reveal the evidence. He doesn't, so Doc spends a moment mixing up the order of the tubes.

'Off you go, leave the flannel.' he says to Hendon, who turns tail immediately. 'Lummox.' Doc says, under his breath, continuing to mix up the results.

'Help yourselves to drinks!' he says, obviously talking to us, though his eyes remain trained on the task at hand.

Nobody is getting a drink; nobody is removing their eyes

from the towel. Eventually he stands, keeping the towel in place.

'Okay, here it is. Your proof!' he exclaims, removing the covering.

He holds the rack aloft, containing the six test tubes. Each containing a sample from the six of us. Five of them are blood red, one is a white, opaque substance.

Avon moves closer, examining the contents. We all follow suit, trying to comprehend. 'Satisfied?' Doc asks to no one in particular.

There's no response.

'The game continues,' he says, placing the rack carefully onto the floor. 'Three groups of two, in the biodome. Alex, pick your partner.'

Alex stops examining the rack and looks at everyone closely. 'Clemence.' she says.

'Very good. Alex and Clemence are group one. Avon, pick your partner please.' Avon looks at me with a wry smile and eyes that suggest I'll owe him one. 'Viola.' he says.

'Avon and Viola are group two. That means Amelia and Cliff are group three.' Doc confirms. Oh Avon you beautiful bastard. You've done me a solid there. We made a pact and now I owe you one on top. Plus, he's gotta spend time with Viola, maybe he feels bad about leaving me at the bar with her. Either way, I'm pleased.

'So,' Doc continues, 'the game is this. You are again invited to take a drink and stroll the gardens in your pair. Group three will pick a member from group two as the most likely machine, group two will pick a member from group one and group one will choose someone from group three. Once you have all cast your votes, I will talk to you about the next steps. Until then, enjoy the views.'

Doc begins to dress while simultaneously gathering up the test tubes and the other medical equipment. It's clumsy but he's making it work. Alex and Clemence have already taken drinks and are cutting their way into the undergrowth.

'You and me then skipper?' Amelia says, passing me a Guinness from the table.

'Aye aye captain, where to?' I reply, jauntily. 'We'll follow those two into the woods.'

Before I can agree with some witty response, she's already heading that way, so I follow. Viola stops us in her tracks.

'So, you're voting for group two, that's me and Avon, I wonder who you'll choose?' she says in a patronising tone.

'Oh, sorry,' Amelia says, equally as vicious, 'I thought you'd know we were gonna vote for you but I guess you're such a major douchebag that you hadn't realised? At least you'll be able to vote for one of us in return, oh no, wait, you can't vote for either of us in return, what a shame.' Amelia smirks and carries on walking; I follow her into the woods.

Chapter Six
An Abundance of Problems.

As we venture from the path and into the woodland, I notice that Amelia doesn't have the usual spring in her step. The mischievous remarks and the playful nature are absent.

As she leads us back towards the trees on the outer edges of the dome where we sat earlier, she doesn't chat or turn back to see if I'm still there.

The temperature has dropped and I can see my breath every time I exhale. The woods are darker than earlier, forcing one to hold a hand out in front, making sure not to walk into a tree, like in a cartoon.

Amelia sits on the same branches as last time and swiftly lights a cigarette. She offers the pack to me, expressionless. Something is on her mind.

I take one, and the lighter, which I use.

Staring out into the darkness, I blow my smoke at the external dome wall, watching it race off in different directions, waiting for her to speak.

'Who did you vote for, Cliff?' she says.

I look at her, she stares blankly into the wilderness. Her

demeanour has completely changed from earlier. Before I can answer, she continues.

'I don't understand how Viola is still here. Agatha, Alex, Avon and you gave the impression that you'd all vote for her. I voted for her so that's five. Then Doc says that the person eliminated has only got three votes and to top that, it's not even her. Now I voted for her, so I know she was one of the people who got two votes. So three of you lied or at least three, maybe Clem voted for her as well and you were all lying? Who did you vote for?'

I briefly consider lying but I can't. 'Agatha.' I utter.

'Why? You gave the impression that you would vote for Viola, coupled with the fact that she's horrible. Agatha wasn't horrible. Why did you pick her over Viola? I don't get it?'

'Look, for the last vote, Avon and I made a pact. We agreed to vote the same way.' 'You said.'

'Well, he went last, it was out of Agatha and Viola, he picked Agatha. I don't know why but we'd agreed so I felt a certain level of loyalty.'

'Loyalty? Everybody is loyal to whoever pays the most. I don't know why he came to that conclusion. Maybe it's tactics. So he voted for Agatha?'

'So he said.'

'So, if we assume that Viola also voted for her, it means that either Clemence, Alex or Agatha did vote for Viola and two of them voted for someone else entirely. I'd love to see Doc's clipboard.' 'Oh to be a fly on the wall.' I say, trying to resuscitate our budding connection.

'Well,' she says, 'Avon isn't here this time, so you're gonna have to be loyal to me.' 'Okay.' I say nervously.

'We're gonna pick Viola but we're gonna discuss each of

them first, so we know where each other is, regarding decisions on everyone else. It's gonna be open, honest and fair. And then we're gonna pick Viola.' she smiles, finally.

I smile back. 'Okay.'

'Right, Avon, thoughts?'

'We're going straight in, are we?' I ask. 'We are.' she confirms.

'I quite like him. Something seems off though, I don't know how to describe it. Maybe he's a bit odd, like, I dunno…I quite like him.' I say.

'When you say that something seems off, I do know what you mean. I also like him but there's an angle. I don't know what his game is. What about Alex?'

'Hang on,' I say, 'what about you? Aren't you going to elaborate on Avon?' 'No. You're going first, then I'll do mine. Alex?'

'Okay, Alex seems pretty cool, nothing suspicious or curious has occurred, I'm not getting a robot vibe.'

'Okay, Clemence?'

I contemplate before speaking.

'She's an interesting one. She started off quite annoying and she got a fair few votes. Now she's not as annoying and slipping back into the crowd, as if she's realised her patterns weren't serving her and has gone about changing them.'

'I know what you're saying but a human might act like that too. I don't think we could hang her for it. What about Viola?'

We look at each other and smile. I scratch my chin. 'She's a witch.'

Amelia laughs.

'No, I think she's a witch Cliff, what do you think?'

'I don't care for her, I don't think she's a machine but, I don't care for her.' I say. 'Okay,' she stares at me, 'so what about me?'

I speak quickly so as to not cause a situation.

'I think you're cool, I think I've got a better connection with you than anyone else here and I…hope you're not a robot!'

She smiles, enjoying the practical compliment.

'Flattery will get you everywhere. So where's your money? Who's the imposter?' I scratch my chin again.

'I really don't know. What about you? Let's hear about your observations.'

She takes the last draw of her smoke and tosses it to the ground, using her foot to smudge it out.

'Okay,' she says, 'but we're voting for Viola this time, regardless?' 'We are.' I nod.

Amelia takes a deep breath.

'This is how I see it. Viola and Clemence are the most unlikely. Both have unlikeable attributes that wouldn't have been programmed into a machine. Avon, though eccentric, has human traits that again, wouldn't have been programmed. Then there's me. I'm alternative, liberal, somewhat outspoken, I drink too much, I smoke too much, I have a lot of bad habits and I don't think they would wire a machine to think and talk like me.'

She pauses and locks eyes with me.

'In my opinion, you and Alex are the most likely. You both sit on the fence like social chameleons, careful not to upset anyone. You're both likeable, they'd make a machine with your qualities, without a doubt. Are you married, Cliff? Or should I say, do you think you're married?' 'Yes.' I say.

'How long have you been married?' 'Twelve years.'

'And are you one of "those" guys?' 'What do you mean, "those?"'

'You know, playing away, being a naughty boy?' 'No, I'm not.' I say.

'Never?'

'Never.'

'That's a shame. I like you. I was hoping we might kiss. To find out if either of us give off any signals that we might be the robot.'

Amelia leans close to me, so our faces are six inches apart. She's clearly waiting for me to speak. She looks beautiful.

'I can't. If I was one of "those" guys, I wouldn't be resisting. I think you're great, I just can't.' I whisper.

She stays locked in position, a siren, sultry and seductively staring into my eyes. I can't believe it. I can feel my integrity weakening, I've never felt like this.

'What if we pressed our lips together, just for a moment, in the name of science, just to know?' It's a barely audible conversation to the outside world but our faces, our mouths are so close, we can hear each other perfectly.

'Know what?'

'Just to know.' she says, inching closer and closer, until our lips gently press together.

We stay, holding the position for several seconds. I close my eyes, a range of emotions flow through me. We don't use tongues and our lips don't really get tense, it's just a soft, tender kiss. Finally, we part, I open my eyes and watch her do the same. We stare at each other, six inches apart. Nothing else exists. The world has stopped. She whispers.

'I think you're real.'

I go to speak but have to swallow first. My throat feels dry. 'You too.' I manage.

Amelia moves back into her spot and lights another smoke, not offering one to me this time.

'Let's go and vote for Viola.' she says, still looking at me with an unhealthy desire. I don't mean to but I'm sure I'm returning the gaze. I'm under a spell.

'Okay.' I say.

We stand and walk towards the main path. She drags from the cigarette and passes it to me. I accept, I guess we're sharing them now.

I've never felt this way so quickly before. We only met a few hours ago and already I have become besotted with her. I'm a married man. I don't accept these feelings anymore.

I make sure, when with a work colleague or acquaintance of some sort, that I don't leave the door ajar. I'll drop into conversation the fact that I'm married and flash my ring about, to ensure that there aren't any misunderstandings and the relationship never has a chance to evolve into anything more.

However, with her, none of my mechanisms are working. I don't know why. I haven't been trying to invite the attraction. Or have I? I don't think I have.

I didn't instigate the kiss. It didn't turn into a full-blown kiss. I have to tell my wife. I will tell her. It just feels like everything here is different. Maybe it's the location or the alcohol or the premise of the evening but tonight feels like a departure from reality.

We pass the smoke back and forth, occasionally giving each a knowing smile, sharing a private happiness.

Now, there is the possibility that one of us is a machine, which changes things. My past, my memories may be entirely fabricated, which somehow makes this situation easier or more acceptable?

If Amelia is the robot, then at least I have been hoodwinked almost, played. Suckered by a woman who is mirroring my taste for her own progression in the game.

However, I don't think she has been this way for the other males here.

As we reach the beginning of the biodome, other guests are drinking and talking amongst themselves. I wonder who will be chosen this time? They're all there, Alex and Clemence will have voted for her or me.

I have time to take a new pint from the table before Doc engages us. 'Have you decided?' he says.

Amelia looks back at me to confirm that I'm not going to throw a spanner in the works. 'Viola.' she says.

He acknowledges and walks to the atrium threshold.

'Everyone, we have a decision. In alphabetical order, Clemence, Cliff and Viola have received the nominations. The three of you will decide which one of you will be safe from the main vote. Alex, Amelia and Avon, follow me to the medical unit. When I return for the other three, you will have decided who to save. Come!'

Doc scrambles away. Alex, Amelia and Avon all look apologetic before charging after him, leaving the three nominees to face each other. Viola addresses the both of us.

'I suppose you voted for me because Amelia insisted and you couldn't say no to her, Avon and I voted for you Clem, because neither of us see Alex as a threat, she doesn't seem to have made any alliances and therefore can be picked off easily. Not exactly robot behaviour. So why did you two vote for Cliff over Amelia?'

Clemence is visibly uncomfortable.

'Alex thinks Amelia is too individual, too alternative to have been specifically programmed that way, I agreed, so Cliff was the only choice we had.

She gives me a sorrowful look. Viola scowls.

'Well I think Amelia is opinionated and forthright, that's why she thinks she can act the way she does.' she says.

'Well, either way,' I say, trying to hide my anger, 'she's not here so we might as well deal with this situation, before Doc gets back.'

'He won't be long; he bloody runs everywhere.' Clemence agrees. 'Well then, let's vote. I vote to save myself.' Viola says, obviously. 'Well, I'm gonna save myself,' I say, 'we're all gonna do that!'

Silence takes over the triumvirate. Clemence struggles with her thoughts, it's etched into her face.

'I'll save Viola.' she says.

I am genuinely astounded. I take a step back, literally and figuratively, a look of confusion swamps my face.

'What?' I muster. Clemence looks at me.

'You don't know what she's been through, she's not the machine. I think that I'm more likely to be the robot than her. You don't understand, you couldn't…'

Mouth agape, I look to Viola. 'Tell me Vi, I don't get it.' She rubs her forehead.

'Okay.' she says, clearly thinking it through.

'You don't have to.' Clemence says to her, gently. Oh man. What is it? Viola speaks to me directly.

'My son was born out of wedlock. Harry and I never married, despite him earning millions and me having the opportunity to tie the money up like a golddigger. He arranged the paperwork anyway so that in the event of anything happening to him, the money, the assets would go to me and Leo, his son. We were in love. It was real. We had so much money that we could go anywhere, do anything, it was…it was amazing. He was an amazing man.'

Her eyes are welling up with tears. I can tell that this story is going to take a turn, what with all the past-tense.

'Leo went to university, studied for seven years and became a doctor. After his final exam, his plan was to come home for a week, before taking his girlfriend to Japan. Two weeks before he came home, my husband went for an MRI scan. He'd been suffering severe headaches for months and had finally been for tests, a typical man, clinging on to ignorant bliss. We got the results a few days later. Brain cancer. Terminal. They gave him three months. With Leo due to arrive in ten days, we decided not to tell him until he returned from Japan. He deserved to be happy after his exams and travelling to the far east and starting a new life, we didn't want to burden him, he'd worked so hard. My husband wasn't visibly ill so we were quite confident of carrying it off in the short term. We didn't tell anyone.'

Viola pauses, coughing gently and composing herself.

'Leo arrived home, we were all so pleased to see each other, it was perfect. He'd arranged to meet a few old friends in the evening at the village pub so we said goodbye and off he went.

The pub was less than a mile away, down a winding, country road. No paths or streetlights. He went on foot and had walked the road a thousand times in his younger days so we weren't really concerned. That night, Harry and I laughed and drank wine and reminisced, it was the first time since the diagnosis that we actually enjoyed time together. Seeing Leo brought memories flooding back and we were both able to reflect on our luck and happiness, I'll never forget. It was the last time I was anywhere near happiness. Leo never came home. Harry went to find him; he came back just before three. Leo was walking back from the pub and was killed by a hit and run. The driver was apprehended the next morning. Also at the pub, drinking, according to witnesses. He was given twelve years but I didn't care about the sentencing, my life was ruined. The health of my husband declined. Our angel was gone. On the morning of our son's funeral, I woke to find that my husband had passed away in his sleep. I went to my son's funeral alone.

Then I had the pleasure of arranging another funeral for another man that I loved. Harry's sister, Bridget, got a lawyer to fight for any assets and financial gain, she hated the idea of the estate going to me. The paperwork we had didn't hold up, and as we weren't married and despite Harry's wishes, she won her day in the sun and I was left with nothing. This was last year. Now I live above a laundromat, working in a coffee shop, remembering how life used to be.'

All three of us are deflated. That sounds awful. Clemence is wearing a sympathetic look, it seems almost patronising but I'm sure she means well.

'I can't be a machine. Why would they programme a backstory like that?'

Viola looks down at the floor, a mixture of shame and despair written in her glazed eyes. 'I'm so sorry.' I say.

'I need to win this game. I can't get my old life back, but I could get something that resembled it, at least.'

'I'll save you, Viola.' Clemence says earnestly.

Viola indicates her approval and looks at me, expecting a similar gesture. 'Does anyone else know this, apart from Clemence and me?' I say.

'I told Alex. She was suspicious of my general disposition so I explained to her why I am the way I am.'

Viola and I are monitoring each other, she's waiting to see if I will also save her, not that my opinion counts for anything if Clemence throws herself under the bus.

I'm trying to decide whether her awful admittance is actually a ruse or not. I'll feel terrible if I vote her out and she's a human but I'll feel duped if I don't vote for her and she's having us all over, spinning a yarn and pulling the wool over my eyes.

Doc returns, saving me from an awkward dilemma. 'Have you reached a decision?'

'Yes.' Viola quickly replies. Doc looks impressed.

'Well, well. I thought this would have to be resolved with "Plan B." Spill the beans then gang, who's safe?'

Viola looks to Clem, inducing her to speak. 'Viola.' Clemence says, firmly.

'Interesting,' Doc says with genuine surprise, 'let's go and shock the others then, come!' He leaves without sprinting off but with pace. Like power-walking.

As we follow him to the others, I start to think about Amelia's reaction, when she discovers who we've agreed to save.

She will be furious.

If Amelia had heard her story, I'm not even sure she would be able to accept it.

Ultimately, the decision is between Clem and me. I think about who the others will vote for. Alex is a mystery; I have no idea what way she will go.

Hopefully, considering the pacts we've previously made, Avon and Amelia will save me.

Viola is another issue. She'll probably save Clem because I didn't crumble after she told me a shocker of a story that was actually her life.

I can be fairly confident but this is a funny old game and in a matter of moments, I could be climbing into a taxi and heading back to my life. Or I could be switched off and put back in the box.

The fast walk to the medical unit is made silently and as we enter the room and Hendon closes the door behind us, the suspense is dominant. The other three, with eyes that are visibly racing back and forth, trying to surmise what the decision has been.

Doc stands before us all and gestures towards Clemence, Viola and me.

'These three have decided to save Viola. The rest of you will choose Clemence or Clifford as the machine. Viola, to avoid an unpleasant tie and as you were saved, you will not be taking part in this vote. An unorthodox, alphabetically backwards vote. Avon, who is the robot?'

Amelia isn't concealing her total disgust, which is directed exclusively at me. Avon is thinking carefully.

'Clemence, sorry.' he says to her.

That's good for me. I'm banking on Amelia to get me over the line but she seems livid. Doc speaks.

'Amelia, who is the robot?'

She shakes her head for several seconds, looking scornfully at me. She can't believe that we've saved Viola. Maybe she would feel differently if she was there, listening to her story. It was tragic.

'Cliff.' she says.

That's really bad. I was kind of expecting that to go my way. I don't know what Alex will do; this could be it.

'One one!' Doc announces, enthused by the drama, 'it's on you Alex, who is the robot?' Everyone in the room studies Alex closely. She looks into the ether, carefully playing it over in her mind. Like a chess player, I imagine she's thinking about three steps ahead and working through the ramifications of her initial decision.

'Clem.' she says.

I exhale, I dodged a bullet. It seems like I want to progress more than I thought. 'Clemence! It's you I'm afraid!' says Doc, readying a needle.

She walks over to the gurney dejectedly, glancing around, emitting a look of disappointment, as if to suggest that we have made a mistake.

Doc goes through the procedure and confirms just that.

'Another human being, this is becoming rather unfortunate gang. Would you like to say anything, Clemence?' he says.

'I've had a lovely time Doc, thank you for your hospitality. I can't believe you guys voted for me; I feel like I've been the most genuine here. I've tried to be authentic and myself, and it's a bit gutting to be honest. I wish you luck in finding this machine, I hope at least one of you gets the opportunity to change your circumstances.' she says.

'Thank you for your involvement! Hendon, please see Clemence safely to her car!' They depart, leaving the five of us facing Doc, waiting for our next disaster.

'The final five! How exciting! Among you is a machine and he we are, you still can't seem to find it!'

He's not wrong. Between miserable guessing and choosing annoying or drunk people to remove, we're no closer to finding the truth. Doc looks absolutely delighted with our hopeless inadequacy.

'Let me remind you, if you guess correctly, you win whatever your heart desires. You're all rich and powerful but it's never enough, I'm sure you all have something missing, something out of reach.'

He obviously isn't aware of Viola's current situation. Unless she's the robot and therefore, he may have dropped a clanger. I'm second guessing everything now though, it's becoming disheartening.

When we arrived earlier, this felt like a fun party game, getting acquainted with strangers and enjoying a few beverages. It doesn't feel like that anymore. The accusations and deceit, dare I say back-stabbing, has turned the evening sour. Mistrust is the overriding feeling.

I look around at the others. Avon and Alex wear looks of ambiguity, Viola looks like a serial killer with the bloodlust for more. Amelia looks angry and at every chance, directs her chagrin at me. I hope I get a moment to explain.

Doc has noticed the tension.

'Okay, follow me to the elevator, I have a rather nice surprise for you all, come.'

He takes a more relaxed gait across the entrance hall and waits for the rest of us as we fill up in the lift. There's more room in here now, which is a good thing, because the space between us is filled with poison.

'Thirteen.' Doc says firmly.

The elevator begins to ascend. 'Where are we going?' Avon asks. 'You'll see.' Doc replies.

Nobody wants to speak in this close proximity and there are some unpleasant scowls being passed around.

Thankfully the lift comes to a stop and the doors part, revealing a magnificent rooftop observatory. Large telescopes are scattered amongst various contemporary art and neoclassical statues. The spherical glass roof allows for a wonderful view of the stars and night sky. At the opposite end, a glass door opens onto a small rooftop garden. Amelia beelines straight over, lighting a cigarette as she exits.

'Enjoy the sights, there's drinks on the table there, take a while, your next decision will come shortly.' Doc says, placing himself in the middle of the room.

Avon goes left to the nearest telescope and with his eye placed on the lens, begins to swoop and swivel with mastery.

Viola helps herself to a drink and sidles next to him.

Alex also helps herself to a drink and follows Amelia into the garden. I watch them discussing something quietly. It's probably about Viola, or me.

Viola and Avon are in discussion now as well, maybe she's telling him about her situation, whipping up more votes in her favour. I need to speak to Amelia and explain myself but with Alex out there, it feels a bit awkward.

I won't have another drink at the moment. It's definitely affecting my clarity and my mind is racing with all of the ramifications.

Feeling rather alone all of a sudden, like a spare prick at an orgy, I spot Doc staring directly at me, smiling like a madman. I have nothing on my plate, so I approach him.

'You look happy.' I say, with a hint of sarcasm.

'I am happy, old boy. The machine is blending in perfectly. Everybody seems too concerned with upsetting each other, it's marvellous!'

He really does seem pleased. 'Do you live here, then?' I say.

'I do. It's not my property, I'm not the owner per se, the company acquired it for research purposes and maintains it for occasions such as this.'

'How long have you been here?'

'About eight years. When my ex-wife fleeced me for everything I had, I moved in here for a short-term fix but as you can see, eight years later…'

'Doesn't the company mind?'

'Certainly not. The more I'm here, the more they can ask of me. Both parties are satisfied. Unlike Amelia, she doesn't appear satisfied. Something you said?'

Doc raises his eyebrows. Of course it was. I saved Viola.

'In the last vote,' I begin, 'Clem and I saved Viola, after she recounted her time leading up to tonight. It was awful. I didn't have the heart to go against it and anyway, Clemence sacrificed her own safety, so there wasn't much I could do.'

Doc continues to smile, he seems to enjoy other people's misfortune, schadenfreude. 'Maybe you should go and talk to her, smooth the waters. She voted for you last time, surprising, considering you two have gotten on ever so well.'

'Did you know about Viola, what's happened to her?'

'Of course, it's part of my job to know how the investors are doing.'

'Then why did you say we were all rich if you knew about her situation, unless you made a slip? Perhaps she's the robot and her financial difficulties wouldn't be relevant; you were maybe addressing everyone else?'

That's taken the smile off of his stupid face.

'Or maybe I didn't want to single anybody out so I was sensitive and careful with my delivery.' '...Maybe.' I say, loaded with suspicion.

Alex leaves Amelia alone in the garden and ventures back into our area. This could be my chance. She approaches Viola and Avon and interjects their conversation. Doc and I watch closely as they converse quietly, covertly. I will go and talk to Amelia.

As I leave Doc and head towards the entrance to the garden, Alex appears by my side. 'We need to talk.' she says.

'I was going to speak to Amelia.' I return. 'Wait, just follow me.'

Alex leads me to a quiet corner of the yard, giving us a perfect view of the garden, where Amelia stands. Viola and Avon have made their way towards her.

'This is it. Watch.' Alex says.

The three of them begin a conversation. I say the three of them, Avon is passively observing, while Viola and Amelia grow more animated and aggressive.

'What's going on?' I ask, without removing my gaze.

'Viola is telling Amelia what's been going on with her life recently. I've just been speaking to Amelia, laying the groundwork, so to speak. I don't think she's going to accept it, she hates Viola.'

'She does.'

We watch them descend into an argument. There's finger pointing and vitriol spewing from both of them. Maybe Amelia will better understand how Clemence and I ended up saving Viola last time. She doesn't appear to be placated though.

'Who are you voting for this time?' Alex asks. 'I'm not sure, you?' I say, remaining guarded.

I don't know Alex that well, I'm not sure where her loyalties lay.

'I haven't decided. Amelia and Viola will vote for each other, so we can control the vote if we agree to vote for one of them.'

'What about Avon?'

'Who knows what Avon will do? He does seem to have a self-preservation though, so I suspect he'll vote for one of those two. You don't need too many brain cells to know they're gonna vote for each other.'

Alex gestures at the madness ensuing in the garden. Hendon has appeared and stands between the two ladies, who are shouting obscenities now.

I'll feel terrible voting for Viola but I like Amelia, I'm not voting for her. Maybe Alex is right though, at this point, it's one or the other.

'Why don't we vote for Viola?' I innocently suggest. Alex purses her lips; they make an unusual noise.

'I was thinking of Amelia. Viola next time. Viola has upset people and Avon wouldn't take much convincing to do it. We'd be the final three. Amelia would be trickier to vote out of the final four. Right now though, she's ripe for the picking. Tactically, Amelia is the correct decision.'

'What about trying to find the robot, you know, the actual point of this game?' I say, attempting to hide my dislike for the idea, despite it having weight.

Alex shakes her head.

'We both know that that's ridiculous. As a group, we haven't been voting for the machine for much of the evening. It's more of a convenient reason to eject people we're not keen on, all the while driven by the human desire to win. Right now, we can be pretty certain that Viola and Amelia will vote for each other because instead of thinking carefully and tactically, they will vote emotionally. Mistakes are always made when your decisions are led by your emotions. The machine among us will never be led in this way. There's a good chance that neither of them are the machine, based on the current climate. Interestingly, Viola tends to vote tactically, it's ruthless. However, I don't think she'll be able to resist this time.'

We watch Hendon physically restrain Amelia, while Avon has a firm grasp on Viola's arm. Needless to say, it's turned ugly. When I say ugly, I mean violent. It's been ugly ever since they met.

'So, if neither of them are the machine, who's your money on?' I ask. Alex continues to watch the drama unfolding.

'Well, I don't think it's me, you're not a bad shout but people are talking about your fondness for Amelia and I don't think a machine would get involved with thoughts of that nature. The jury's out but I've had an eye on Avon since we arrived and my suspicions have only grown stronger as the numbers have dwindled. What about you?'

'Well, what you're saying makes sense. I agree that Avon is a strange character…why don't we vote for him, I mean, couldn't you persuade Viola to get him out? We could all win.' I say.

'It's not gonna happen, dear, sweet Cliff. There's five people left and those two are voting for each other. Going for Avon now, complicates the game. In fact, at this stage, Avon is safe, as am I. The only other play at this point, and you won't like it, is you. When I was with Amelia there, she didn't have a kind word to say and kept referring to you as "Judas", so if I said that I was voting for you, despite her hatred for Viola, she may be swayed. Avon has a tendency to say your name, Viola seems to steer votes and if she knew we were calling you, she wouldn't hesitate. You see where this is going.'

'So, in this round, I'm the back-up plan?'

'You are, you're the obvious choice. Don't sweat it though, Amelia and Viola are killing each other, all we have to do is help them along. Amelia seems the more affable of the two, so she's gotta go next, we might not get a better opportunity.'

'But if we both vote for Avon, we'd only need to convince one of them to do the same and that'd be that.' I offer.

Alex smiles.

'You really don't wanna vote for her! Amelia wouldn't sway her vote from Viola to Avon, the only one she'd swap for, and even that is unlikely, is you. Viola sees Avon as her closest ally left, so that's never gonna happen. It's Amelia.' she replies with certainty.

'Why don't we vote for Viola then?' I feel like we've been down this road but I'm getting desperate.

'Look, if we get Viola out and there's four of us left, what happens next? I'm not sure. If we get Amelia out and there's four of us left, what happens next, we've got Viola to fall back on.

Actually, she'd be ideal for coming third. It would guarantee us making the final. We could agree to vote for Amelia, then get Viola to vote for Avon, although that would be tough, maybe we could all vote for you in the next round. Then get Avon to vote out Viola in third, mind you, they're becoming pally so they might vote me out…'

Alex is thinking aloud and seemingly working the tactics through. I'd say she might be the robot but she's snookering herself with overplaying and baffling predictions that are out of her control. In the garden, Hendon is escorting Amelia away and Avon is calming Viola down. Doc has the smile back on his face, enjoying the riot.

'The other stages of the game are difficult to predict but this time, it's definitely Amelia. It's the right decision. I'm gonna speak to Avon, get it done.' Alex is assured.

Hendon helps Amelia into the lift and they disappear behind the closing doors. Doc looks directly at Alex and me.

'Now might be a good time to venture back to the gurney and take a vote. I'll grab the others…' He quickly steps out into the garden and gives instructions to the other two.

Alex and I slowly walk to the elevator and take our places. Doc enters next, grinning as he does. I'm not sure Alex will get a chance to speak with Avon in private, we're going down to make a decision now. I can't vote for Amelia, can I? She'll feel so betrayed. I understand Alex's theory but my integrity is calling. I'll vote for Viola, it's the right thing to do. Maybe I'll vote for Alex, that'd put a cat amongst the pigeons?

Viola and Avon enter the lift and find a spot. Neither glance at me. Doc speaks and the elevator descends.

'Avon?' Alex says.

I can't believe it. I think she's going to accost him in front of the rest of us. I know Amelia isn't here but blimey, this feels unscrupulous.

He turns and looks at her.

'Have you decided who to vote for?' she asks.

He's visibly uncomfortable and wincing. She isn't deterred.

'You know who to vote for, it makes sense. Viola, Cliff and I are gonna vote for her, that's the only choice at this point.'

Avon scowls. He looks unsure. I don't know why she's assuming that I'm voting for her. I decide to say nothing though, I'm not comfortable with Doc being in earshot when discussing things. I don't know why.

'I'm not sure.' Avon manages. Viola chimes in.

'Not sure? She was aggressive out there, you were there! After everything I've been through, you'd think she could hold her tongue but no! She couldn't help herself. Having digs and effing and jeffing! It's time for her to leave, robot or not! What on earth aren't you sure about?'

Avon closes his eyes and rubs his forehead. 'I don't think she's a robot.'

Alex picks up the rope.

'It's her time, that's what it is. If you don't vote for her, you may not get another chance. She's popular here, I like her, but it is what it is. It's the right call.'

The elevator doors slide open and the five of us plod across the hall and into the medical unit. Amelia and Hendon are waiting for us, both standing near the gurney. Not sitting on the gurney. She looks down at the floor so it's difficult to see the look of contempt on her face.

I'm not sure how this'll go. If Avon and I vote for someone else, Amelia might be safe. I haven't had the chance to talk to her since the Viola incident and feel awful about it.

She clearly thinks I'm a turncoat and I don't want that to be her lasting impression of me, we were getting on so well. I think she liked me. I'm sure she did. I want that feeling again.

The tension in the room is evident. This feels like a big decision.

During this evening, I've learnt that, despite people telling you what they'll do, who they'll vote for, you never really know until the moment they say the name.

Sometimes it's the name they said it would be. Other times it isn't and you discover that there's been a secret collusion, unbeknownst to you, where others have agreed to do this or that, after they've agreed to do this or that with you. It's horrendous and despicable.

Doc stands before us, waiting for the din to subside. Hendon covers the exit. The order in which we're called to vote will be pivotal.

'Okay. That was exciting. Now it's time to vote out who you think is the robot. I will choose you all in a random order to ensure fairness. Three votes are required for elimination.'

It won't be random. He saw the chaos; he'll rig it for the cameras. 'Viola, you're first. Who is your vote for?' he says.

'Amelia.' she replies, without hesitation.

'Okay, Amelia, you're next. Who is your vote for?' 'Viola.' comes the reply. Doc was still speaking.

'Okay, it's one each for Amelia and Viola. Alex, who is your vote for please?'

Alex glances thoughtfully at the four of us, trying to work out the various ramifications. Finally, she apologises and while looking straight at her, says 'Amelia.'

Doc allows a quiet moment, making sure the brevity is hitting home, before saying what I've been dreading.

'Cliff, who is your vote for?'

I look down sheepishly, a quick glance around the room confirms my suspicions. All eyes are on me. I decide to pick my heart over my head, for a change.

'Viola.' I say.

Chapter Seven
The Business End.

'Two each for Amelia and Viola. A vote now for Alex or Cliff would be inconsequential and leave us back here so, Avon, who will you vote out, Amelia or Viola?' Doc delivers the words powerfully in an attempt to stoke the drama.

Avon strokes his chin and stares between the two. It feels like an eternity passes until, he begins nodding his head, as if comfortable with his decision.

'Amelia.' he says.

Already standing next to the gurney, she offers her arm, the expression on her face doesn't change from disappointment.

'Amelia is out!' Doc exclaims, taking a sample from her arm and running it through the machine. 'Would you like to say anything?' he asks her.

Amelia shakes her head slowly, the fire in her eyes raging. She's clinging on to her emotions, managing to keep a lid on her ire.

'Human!' he announces, holding the evidence aloft. 'Hendon, do the honours.'

Hendon walks Amelia from the room. She doesn't offer me a

look or a sideways glance, she's gone. I can't believe it. Like a half-completed jigsaw puzzle, it felt like our friendship was progressing but unfinished. I'm gutted. We didn't have a chance to say our goodbyes or exchange numbers. I may never see her again. She was a human all along. I probably won't see her again. I will remember her but memories fade. They just do.

Doc looks slowly around at the four of us.

'Early this morning, some of the scientists invited me to place a bet. They had placed money on how many of our guests would remain this evening when they successfully guessed the machine. They hadn't held out much hope for their machine and thirteen, eleven, nine and eight were their predictions. I was mocked and jeered when my money went on four but look at me now. Regardless of the outcome, I will have guessed the closest. I found the machine to be remarkably uncanny, its self-learning ability is something we can't fully understand. Follow me to a room we haven't seen before and I will tell you the reason why I stand before you, the reason why the progress of artificial intelligence has become my life's work, come!'

Doc leaves the room at a normal pace and the rest of us follow, Hendon closes the door behind us and brings up the rear.

We are led through the entrance hall and a long way down one of the corridors. We go well past rooms that we have previously entered and take a few left and right turns. Eventually, Doc enters a door that reveals a stairwell and leads us down into the bowels.

We reach the basement level, it's dingy but tidy.

Doc goes to a door opposite the stairs. He takes a big bunch of keys from his pocket and deftly finds the correct one. After a turn and click, he opens the door, revealing darkness.

Casually reaching around and turning on the lights, Doc stumbles forward, as the light shudders into existence.

'Welcome to the cutting room!' he shouts.

As we follow him in, the lights begin to settle, letting us see what's actually going on.

It's not like any of the other rooms we have been in. It's a large room with hardwood floors, like a basketball court. However, stacked floor to ceiling is computer equipment. Some items are recognisable and some items are alien. It's a robot graveyard. Small pathways run here and there and as we are led along one, I'm reminded of picking out a Christmas tree from an outdoor sale, where they have too much stock and not enough room. You can't see anything apart from what's directly in front of you. It's like a bomb has gone off.

Doc takes us into an opening, which is set up with just enough room for five chairs and a stand-up hard drive with four beer bottles on.

'Please, take a seat, help yourself to a drink.' he says, sitting down himself.

As Hendon steps into the opening, his body shape brushes a poorly placed monitor, which brings down a wall of equipment and wires all over the floor. We all watch nervously, hoping that the loose gear won't bring everything else around us tumbling down. There're a few groans from teetering electricals but they hold in place. The rest of us carefully sit in the chairs, Viola and I help ourselves to a drink and await Doc's orders.

'Dear oh dear.' he says, clearly directing his shameful head shake at Hendon. Hendon grimaces apologetically and Doc turns his attention back to business.

'When I was sixteen, I studied science, among other things,

at college. I was considered a bright boy and excelled in chemistry. I enjoyed it and received offers to further my education from all across the country. While I was there, I took a night job at a factory that made pastries. Cheese twists were my favourite, although I enjoyed anything that was surrounded by pastry. My specific job was order entries. I would input data into a computer, say, this company wanted five of one item and six of another. In front of me was a glass container with three robotic arms inside. A conveyor belt would run the various pastry products down and the information I had entered would tell the arms which products to use. They would all have a different order to pick and they

would reach down and one by one, take the items they needed and drop them into a box in front of them carefully, thus preparing the correct order. The boxes also arrived on a conveyor belt so that production could continue at speed. When an order was completed, the arm would press a button and the box would roll to its next destination, immediately replaced by an empty carton.

The process would start again quickly and this would continue for hours. I would spend forty minutes inputting the data into the computer, assigning the arms with their tasks, then I would turn the machine on and watch it burn. It was fascinating and there began my educational shift from chemistry to robotics and specifically, after a peculiar incident occurred, the idea of

free-thinking machinery.'

Doc looks around to make sure we're suitably attentive. We are.

'I was there for two years, the arms were installed two years before I arrived and according to colleagues, had never made mistakes or displayed any unusual behaviour. At the tail end of my first shift, arm one, known affectionately as Fester, did something that has remained in my thoughts to this day.'

He looks at our faces again, seeing if he's managed to conjure up any excitement.

'After an eight hour shift during the night, tiredness had crept in and perhaps I wasn't as focused as I had been in the earlier part of my shift. I was watching the arms going through their monotonous instructions when Fester reached out and picked up a pastry and just held it there, above the conveyor belt, as if wondering what to do next. Of course, I sat upright and began frantically looking at my computer screens. Nothing was flashing red and the printouts continued in formation. I looked around for a colleague who might be able to explain but there wasn't anyone there. Fester brought the pastry towards me and placed it down next to the box. He then hovered back into position and continued his task. Occasionally swooping in and plucking the next pastry for his order. He went back to uniform. It was an anomaly. I checked the order on the screen, that Fester was assembling, it was correct, the instructions inputted were correct, so I assumed that perhaps he had taken the wrong item and discarded it. Then I thought how ridiculous it was to think that; he was a robot following human instructions and the option to discard items isn't built into the data. We continued as normal for ten minutes until the shift was over, then I switched off the machinery and checked the contents of the rejected pastry. Its ingredients were the vegetarian option, cheese, tomato and basil. There were twenty required for this particular order, so the only plausible explanation was that Fester had already fulfilled that line and had accidentally taken an extra by mistake. Colleagues had assured me that the arms didn't make mistakes, so I continued down the rabbit hole. I took the box that was being filled by Fester and investigated. It appeared that he had picked the order correctly, from top to bottom, the last line was the vegetarian option and so far, he had taken thirteen. So he needed that particular pastry for his order but chose to reject it, even though he had no built-in code to make that kind of decision. Exasperated, I went home. I may have been tired and although I was sure I hadn't imagined it, I may have exaggerated it in my mind somehow. I couldn't stop thinking about it though.'

'That is strange.' says Viola, taking a sip of her drink. 'It gets stranger.' Doc assures her.

'I discussed it with peers over the next week, we went through the systems and performed diagnostics but found nothing. Fester was working at top capability and the problem was considered an anomaly. There were even disparaging comments regarding the truth of my confession and I was cast out by my colleagues somewhat, eating my lunch alone and not being invited to Friday drinks and birthday shenanigans.'

I can quite imagine Doc being an outsider in most situations, he's obviously eccentric. He looks a bit downcast after revealing that information though, he was a young man, probably hopeful of fitting in and finding friendship. We've all been there.

'A few months passed without incident, everything running like clockwork. I was naturally feeling isolated and became closer to the three robots on my station. Talking to them and browsing their code to feel like I knew them. It was a bit sad really.'

Doc blows his nose, studying the floor, unable to meet our gaze.

'It was a Friday. Just before the end of the shift. Fester did it again. I was watching them more intently and it confirmed to me that I wasn't going mad or telling tall tales. At the shift's end, I checked through the order and once again, Fester had disregarded an item needed for his task. It was as if he was being playful or mischievous with me, toying with me. I considered telling my supervisor but what if the same thing happened again? They already questioned the validity of my previous account. This time I decided to keep it to myself but ran my own diagnostics in the background, trying to find an answer to the quandary. In electronic components there is always a reason why something responds the way it does. The answer is in the code or the equipment, it can't just do that of its own volition. I spent weeks inspecting the codes, the data, analysing everything, over and over, until I felt I had exhausted every avenue. Then, Fester did it again.

No harm was caused, he was picking the orders correctly, completing his tasks efficiently. There just wasn't a rhyme or reason to it. Over the two years that I was there, Fester did this sixty-six times. I recorded the dates and times, never telling my coworkers. Occasionally I would have holidays and a colleague would take over my role, but I never heard of any incidents that happened in my absence. I began to think that without any glitches in the code or robotics and no unusual activity in my absence, that the only common denominator in this curious case, was me. And I was fully aware that any suggestion, even the thought of it, was crazier than anything else, so when I left the company with a smile and a handshake, I took my thoughts with me.'

I glance around to see that everyone is captivated by the story, you could hear a pin drop. Even Hendon has lost his distant glare.

'I went to Bristol University, adding engineering and robotics to my curriculum, and later dropping chemistry altogether. Chemistry would be considered a hard science and although I was considered competent, I just wasn't giving it the time or attention it required. I fell in with three second year students, who were working on a project that ticked every box in my inquisitive column. They had designed two, very industrial looking arms with grab claws for hands, that were positioned three feet high, three feet apart, in a nine by nine foot, glass container. Every two minutes, a funnel that was positioned at the top of the container would release two tennis balls, directly at the claws. The students were attempting to essentially, catch the balls in the claws. The balls would fall into the palms, but the trick was to get the fingers to react to the impact and close around the ball, thus catching. Needless to say, at the end of each session, one of us would have to open the cabinet and collect all of the failed tennis balls, returning them to the funnel box. Imagine opening a loaded-up cupboard under the stairs, where everything starts falling out around you, it was like that.'

Doc is more jovial now; I get the impression that he has fond memories about this time in his life.

'We would often go to the pub and pick over the bones of our failures, trying new ideas out on each other and agreeing on the next direction to success. It was a healthy group to be a part of. We would cancel trips home to see our folks and blow off social engagements to spend more time holed up in the lab with our claws and our ideas and our youthful exuberance. Patrick and Stephen had created an arm each so there was always a healthy competition but we would share our ideas and help each other, it was always amicable, teamwork makes the dream work. Hayley would supply extra code to both arms and provide the music. She would often play grunge or rap or electronic music. Classical…All sorts really. The soundtrack to our experience. She was more outgoing than the other two, you could say that she provided street smarts to the group, although there wasn't much competition. I would go between the three of them, helping where I could and learning, listening, cutting my teeth in that environment. I found it exhilarating to be honest.'

The nostalgia has gripped Doc and he's firing now.

'Of course, a love triangle was evident and threatened to destroy the relationships and more importantly to me, the project. Patrick clearly had feelings for Hayley, who in turn had feelings for Stephen. Stephen had a long-distance girlfriend from his town and he would say that they would often speak on the phone but the rest of us secretly doubted her existence.'

'What about you?' Alex asks.

'I had feelings for Hayley but being a year younger, I don't think we enjoyed anything other than friendship. I was too immature for her, she would occasionally date the older students, even a teacher at one point but I digress.'

Doc takes a deep breath.

'It was Patrick's birthday. November Twenty-ninth. We met, as we often did, after lessons, in laboratory four, where our experiment room was hidden away at the end of the science block. After a shop run for booze and balloons, a music birthday playlist and some code preparation, we began running our experiment. At four minutes after nine, the robotic arm that Patrick was operating, successfully, incredibly, caught the tennis ball. He saw it happen, the rest of us were at our stations, half-cut and staring into space but the evidence presented itself. The claw held the ball tightly, without instructions regarding what to do next. We gathered around the birthday boy as he typed his keyboard rigorously, telling the claw to release and await the next target. It did so and after an intense thirty second wait, the next tennis ball exited the funnel and dropped towards the claw. It felt like slow motion as the claw grasped it and held firm. It caught it again. It wasn't a fluke. We ran the test another seven times, the claw catching every one. Pure elation mixed with alcohol produced a series of high-fives, embraces, inappropriate kissing. We agreed to turn the lights out and go to the pub to celebrate our long overdue achievement.'

Doc is starting to become more emotional and rueful; I sense that this story is going to take a turn.

'It was a jubilant hour; we were all heady with pride and intoxication. Well, we decided to go to *Club Orange*. A late night drinking establishment that played alternative rock and dance music. The dance floor was alive with young flesh and the underground club smelt of testosterone and possibility. We began drinking and dancing. I wouldn't normally dance, my self-awareness and general inability to look like I know what I'm doing stops me but in there, it was different.

Anyway, at one point, Hayley and Patrick went to get drinks. Stephen beckoned me to the arcade room, which was slightly quieter. He began talking about the experiment and it was clear

that he was holding a grudge, struggling to hide his animosity towards Patrick. Struggling to understand how Patrick, an inferior engineer in his opinion, had managed to garner a better arm than he, an arm that had successfully achieved its task. Stephen considered Patrick to have been arrogant that evening, and despite my protestations, mainly centred around his birthday, Stephen would confront him, even assault him. I tried to reason with Stephen, take the edge off, but his internal dialogue was in complete control. He was a big lump and had previously boxed for his county, Patrick on the other hand, was a slip of a chap. Short and slight. Now, I'm a big believer of "It's not the size of the dog in the fight, it's the size of the fight in the dog." However, I don't think Patrick had fight in him. He was a lover, a pacifist. As I tried to come up with another reason to prevent the potential disaster, my shoulder was grabbed and I'm spun around. Hayley passes me a drink, tells Stephen that Patrick is bringing his one and then proceeds to drag me through the crowds, back up the entrance stairs and out into the smoking shed. In those days I would smoke to try and fit in, most people did smoke, unlike these days. Hayley lit two cigarettes and passed me one. I've got news! she said. So have I, I replied.

Me first, she began. I'm basically gonna go and tell Stephen how I feel. I've liked him for a while, I'm sure you've noticed. I'm thinking, we got the experiment to work, we're all happy, I should go for it.

What about his girlfriend? I said. Well, she said that his talk of having a girlfriend was probably bollocks. A ploy to make us all impressed. I agreed there was no evidence but couldn't stop thinking about what was currently happening inside, between Stephen and Patrick.'

'Oh my god, what happened?' Viola says.

'I had to think fast, I didn't want the situation to become even more complex. I told Hayley I would go in first and distract Patrick so that she could speak to Stephen alone, knowing full well that I might have the chance to prevent an altercation. I rushed down the stairs, scanning the room carefully. The place was packed, and the dark lighting made it impossible to distinguish anything that was further away than an arm's length in front of you. The music was pounding, I couldn't hear myself think. I began to laboriously push my way around the throng, to no avail. I clambered to the bar and looked along it. Patrick stands at the end, looking cheerful, waving at me to join him, so I do. He asks me if I've seen Stephen. I say no. He says he's looked everywhere for him, maybe he's gone home. I nod in agreement. I'm hoping he has gone home. Five minutes ago, he was set to tear Patrick limb from limb. Patrick is acting excited and tells me he has a plan. He's taken some drugs in the toilet and he feels great. He thinks it was cocaine. I'm going out of my mind with anxiety after all of these revelations when he tells me that he is in love with Hayley and will tell her when he sees her next. His arm caught a ball, it's his birthday, he's drunk and high, what could possibly go wrong? Well, Hayley joins us at the bar, asking where Stephen is. Patrick tells her that he went home, he doesn't mention that this is merely an assumption and invites her to the arcade room, where it's quieter. He beckons me along too, I've no idea why but follow anyway.'

'This is crazy.' Alex says, under her breath.

'Patrick begins to unleash a barrage of feelings at an unsuspecting Hayley. How he's been pining over her since they became friends, he's lovelorn, desperate almost, for these feelings to be returned. He has always felt it was unrequited but had to tell her, hopeful of a similar retort. First of all, he has said all this to her with me standing right there, not even in earshot but right there, as part of the conversation. Secondly, Hayley, as gently as possible, has to let him down

easily. She doesn't share these feelings and sees the relationship as a purely platonic one. Watching his face sink and melt into his shirt was horrible but I knew that it would happen. The nature of this threesome and their affections for each other were fairly apparent to someone in my position. Patrick offered an understanding smile but looked absolutely heart-broken. He trudged to the toilet, Hayley looked shyly at me and raced to the stairs, leaving me standing alone, wondering what would happen next? And what should I do? I don't fancy following Patrick to the toilet, I don't know what to say to Hayley and where's Stephen? Maybe I could just go home, it's technically nothing to do with me? So I sipped my pint and pondered the next move.'

Doc glances around to make sure nobody is asleep. We're not, we're all totally invested in the outcome.

'So, I think it couldn't get any worse, which of course was a mistake. It was about to get far worse. I look across the dancefloor, the sea of bodies begins to separate and Stephen walks towards me, looking agitated. I say agitated, I'm understating it somewhat, he looks livid. Before I can accost him, he plants a right hook across my jaw. His fist feels like a bowling ball and I hit the ground quickly and efficiently. He stands over me, pointing and shouting obscenities. The music, combined with the ringing in my ears, drowns most of it out, but I do catch the odd f-word. At this point, I haven't even attempted to stand back up, I'm down for the count and although not unconscious, completely incapacitated. I see bouncers and other security staff tackle Stephen and drag him towards the exit. He's putting up a fight and it's getting quite physical. Then they disappear through the hall and up the stairs. I'm left on the floor, a hot mess. A fellow reveller is asking me if I'm okay and I'm slurring back a noise that is supposed to sound like the word no but doesn't sound much like anything coherent. He helps me up, but my legs are jelly so three of the crowd collapse me into a seat. One of them hands me a bottle of water, which I drop immediately. My brain is slowly grasping responses but it's not there yet. I sit there, gathering my thoughts, the three revellers seem to think I'm okay and go back to their fun. The next thing I know, Patrick stands before me, asking what happened. I manage to slur Stephen's name and point at my jaw, indicating my plight. He tells me that Stephen was accusing him of acting high and mighty and lording it over him this evening. He told Stephen that it was his birthday and anyway, perhaps it's because Doc has been stroking his ego, telling him that he's better than Stephen and was always going to create a better arm. It explained why Stephen attacked me. Unfortunately it was complete nonsense. Patrick was apologetic but I sensed he was pleased to dodge the bullet. He offered to help me to a taxi, which I was grateful for, as I could barely walk. He and a bouncer took me through the club and across the road, to the taxi rank. I don't really remember what happened after that but I woke up in my own bed. I stumbled to the mirror to see if my face was marked, my head was throbbing and swallowing was tricky. Bowling ball was an accurate description, the entire left side is black and blue, I look awful. I spent the rest of the weekend convalescing and eating through a straw.'

'Patrick was out of order.' Alex says. 'He was.' Avon agrees.

'I stayed at home on Monday and Tuesday, in constant pain. Giving me plenty of time to work out how to deal with Patrick and Stephen. I felt honesty was my best play with Patrick as far as him telling Stephen that it was me who was responsible for inflating his ego on that fateful night. It was a false accusation and if he didn't put Stephen straight then I would. I went in early on Wednesday, to see if our lab was affected by the weekend's debauchery. Hayley was there already, looking solemn. I could tell that she'd cried. She informed me that during Stephen's brawl with the bouncers, he had hit his head on the curb outside and died instantly. Patrick had put the word about that it was after an altercation with me. I told her that it wasn't so much of an altercation, it was Stephen walking over and decking me because Patrick had told him that I didn't rate his scientific nous and I was lauding Patrick for his success. Hayley didn't know what to believe, she just looked blankly ahead. I notice, as I navigate the university complex, that other students looked at me disdainfully and with my bruised jaw, I looked the part, responsible somehow for Stephen's death. Patrick kept up the facade that I and not he was involved in the fallout, coupled with taking the acclaim as the main player in our project success. I was not invited, nor welcome at the funeral. Only Patrick went from our group, even speaking during the eulogy. Hayley stopped coming to the classes and left the university altogether a few weeks later. Patrick was touted as the next big thing in robotics and spoke to many suitors, all wanting to grab onto the coattails of his rising star. Ultimately, he left to finish his degree on the job, being paid an exorbitant amount of money for his age and skill set. It all turned out rather well for Patrick, his favourable outcome, only exceeded by a new found arrogance. I was left in the lab alone, with only Stephen's arm for conversation. Over the next school year, I worked on it every evening, every weekend, trying to emulate our previous accomplishment. I was focused and relentless, seldom eating and rarely sleeping. After six months, the arm could catch balls. Over the following two months, I had it throwing, dropping, selecting balls from four different receptacles in which to release them. My achievements were revered and the offers for future employment came thick and fast, however, it always felt overshadowed by Patrick and his pursuit to the top of our profession. I wasn't jealous, or maybe part of me was but, my main grudge was the good fortune. I felt he was in a privileged position because of luck, with a splash of "throwing me under the bus" mixed in. As I progressed over the next several years, I would watch his moves closely, as he was becoming something of a poster boy for the advancements in robotic engineering. I always seemed one step behind. Less than. We would occasionally accept invitations to social events in our field and I would see him there. I would try to engage him with a nod or a smile or a friendly wave. He would look through me and generally give me a wide berth. Avoidance. I suppose that when he saw me, it would bring up all the memories from that time in his life and how he metaphorically jumped in a boat and drove off, leaving the rest of us to drown in the sea. Stephen died, Hayley disappeared and I was the scapegoat. Patrick strode from the wreckage with everybody wanting a piece of his shit.'

Doc is clearly holding on to his grudge.

'Then, one day in Spring, I had a job interview with The

Krelboyne Institute. They were looking for a designer of robotic joints and I ticked enough boxes to cruise the meeting. I was offered the job on the spot and a large sum of money to keep me warm at night. I was walking on air, it felt like I was finally getting to the head table. When I got home, I turned the news on and saw that Patrick had died, lung cancer, thirty-three. A memorial service was held the week after. I went and as we all sat there, listening to people wax lyrical about how extraordinary he was, I felt nothing. I was there to rub shoulders with his people and to try and extract hard cash, persuading them to support my venture, now that the great man was gone. I felt it was my duty to avenge Stephen and Hayley, to take back what was rightfully theirs. Ours. He took the limelight for himself and now karma would return after his death, courtesy of me. It was an unhealthy obsession. It is an unhealthy obsession. I didn't want to publicly slay him and attempt to turn people against him, it mightn't work. Far better to do what he did and keep secret the devilment I was partaking in. I easily secured most of his investors by saying the right things.

Then I persuaded his widow to leave the home in which they lived as it was likely to stir up painful memories. I was tempted to court her and really walk in his shoes but she wasn't interested and besides, she was more than happy to take the money and run. They didn't have children and she was an attractive woman in her late twenties. She could start her life again, this time with a fat wallet. The house is of course, this house that we sit in now.'

He seems pleased with himself but this is a fucked up story. It isn't normal behaviour.

'I thought it was the perfect place for our experiments and the company was looking for a large, isolated manor that we could work in privately, so this complex was an easy sell. Ever since then, I have found the right team to produce the impossible. People are concerned about the rise of the machines but while the threat lives inside computers, it seems manageable. Until we can produce a robot that looks like a human, with the capacity of a machine, it will always feel like a distant threat. People prefer something tangible and I think we have it. One of the four of you is that very thing. Indistinguishable. Hidden in plain sight. Perfect? Maybe.'

'What happened to Hayley?' Viola asks.

'That's one piece of the story I can't give you. I thought about contact many times over the years but never looked. It is a regret; I think of her most days. I just can't do it. What's done is done.' He looks reflective and rueful. It's a shocking story and nobody is saying anything. We're all looking around awkwardly, waiting for Doc to collect himself. Finally, he does.

'Well, that's enough of that. I don't want to prattle on and dampen the spirits, we're having a wonderful evening so let's continue our quest. I think as we have equal numbers regarding gender, we'll have girls against boys. Alex, Viola, you will follow me back to the unit and choose one of the boys to face the vote. Avon, Cliff, I will return to collect you, you will do the same.

Once we're all there, the game will commence. Girls, come!'

Doc springs from his seat and leads them away at pace. Avon and I exchange glances and both lean forward in our respective seats.

Chapter Eight
The End of The Beginning of The End.

'He won't be long; I'm thinking ten minutes. We better make the decision.' Avon says sternly. 'I know, especially considering he virtually runs everywhere.'

Avon gives me a half smile but is clearly concentrating on the task at hand.

'Here's what I think,' he says, 'I think we need to try and work out who they'll vote for, so we can choose the correct female to play against their choice.'

'So if they choose you,' I say, 'who would be your ideal opponent?'

'Alex. Viola could convince you to vote for Alex instead of me. However, if you're chosen and we pick Alex, I think Viola would want you out. I could try and persuade her but I don't think she'd turn.'

'Well that seems risky. What if we vote for Viola?' I say, trying to grasp the tactical analysis. Avon rubs his temples.

'Well, on the face of it, it seems the most obvious play. I think either of us could convince Alex to vote for her, there may not be much persuading to be fair. However, there are two issues with it.' 'Which are?'

'Number one, Viola is the least popular person left. If she makes the final three, she will be ganged up on and voted out, no problem. So if we vote for her now and they vote for one of us, it will be a wonderful opportunity to vote one of us out instead, eliminating the competition, maybe even finding the machine?'

I consider this and understand the thinking, if we vote for Viola and they vote for Avon, Alex could easily sway me into getting rid of him there and then and ganging up on Viola next time. Therefore, I can accept that maybe he would do the same. He's pretty much admitted that if we vote for Alex and they vote for me, he wouldn't stop Viola from kicking me out.

'And number two?' I ask.

'She probably isn't the machine. Technically it would be seen as another wasted vote.' 'Unless she is the machine?' I say, playing devil's advocate.

'It's so unlikely. Her personality is telling.' he replies with certainty.

We both sit quietly, weighing up the options. I decide to show my hand.

'Are you saying that if we vote for Alex and they vote for you, Viola and I would save you?' 'Yes.'

'But if we vote for Alex and they vote for me, Viola and you wouldn't save me?' 'That's correct. Viola wouldn't change her mind, she's after you.'

'Couldn't you plant a seed, something inventive?' 'I could try but…' he tails off.

'Well, look Avon, from my perspective, I want to vote for

Viola, you understand? It's less risky, for me anyway.'

'I understand.' Avon replies. 'So what about you?' I ask.

'Well, the truth is, I still think it's you but I can't vote for you at this point. If we vote for Alex, I think Viola would save me, so that's my opinion.'

'But if they vote for me and I'm against Alex, I'll lose. We have to decide between us two, Doc will return soon and we've got a split decision. Let me say this.'

Avon watches me intently.

'Throughout this evening, Viola has sidled up to certain people to do her bidding. Clemence was the most recent, I saw it first-hand. When push comes to shove, she drops them like a hot potato. Who's to say she isn't doing the same thing with you? If they put you up and we choose Alex, Viola might see it as a great opportunity to nudge you out. In fairness, both Alex and I have an eye on you for the machine, so neither of us would put up much of a fight. If we choose Alex, the potential risks are significant. If we choose Viola, it's a much higher likelihood that both of us will progress to the final three.'

Avon is mulling it over, stroking his eyebrows and rubbing his hairline. Eventually, he begins to slowly nod his head.

'Okay.' he says reluctantly.

'Okay?' I say, looking for a more certain confirmation.

'Okay,' he says, 'but if you and Alex think it's me, this could be my best chance of keeping Viola in the final three, maybe you and Alex will vote me out in third place. Maybe my best chance of heads up will be if Viola is still in?'

'We'll cross that bridge when we come to it, but you could be eliminated now if we don't go for Viola?' I counter.

'I still think she'd keep me in over either of you.' he tries. 'Think or hope?'

He rubs his face with both hands, clearly divided. I give it one more plea.

'It's simple really Avon. If we choose Alex, we've both got the potential to lose. If we choose Viola, we've both got the potential to win.'

He nods along.

'I wish we knew who they were picking.' he says with a grimace. 'I know.'

'Okay, we'll vote for Viola and between the three of us, we'll see where the chips fall.' he says. 'Okay.' I say.

Right on cue, the sound of Doc heaving between machinery gets closer. Avon and I share a look of agreement. Doc enters the makeshift opening.

'Hello again! Follow me to the unit. The ladies have aligned their vote, I trust you've done the same?'

We both nod.

'Marvellous,' he says, 'Giddyup!'

With that, he disappears back along his chosen path, Avon and I follow the sounds of grunting until we're reunited in the hallway.

Along the way, Doc talks to us about the job he had as a teenager, the one with the mischievous robot arms that would occasionally defy logic and do things that they weren't programmed to do. He says that he went back there, years later, to look over the blueprints and run diagnostics on the machinery. He felt that there were some mechanics, specifically the arm joints, that could improve the project that he was currently working on. When asking them about the glitches he experienced when under their employ, he was told that there was never another case, before or since, of people reporting a similar incident. Doc told us that there was nothing in the blueprints pertaining to the unusual behaviour and that nobody else had experienced what he had experienced, leading him to one conclusion. That the only differential was him. He became fixated on this, somehow thinking that the robotic arm knew that he was present and solely began to tease him and taunt him with unexpected mannerisms. No one else. Just him. He knew it couldn't be true but with no other explanation, he had nothing else to grasp on to. It came close to destroying him and although he has his emotions about it under control, he thinks about it daily. He appears wistful as we enter the unit. Alex and Viola watch the three of us closely as we approach and stand opposite them in the centre of the room. Doc snaps out of it. 'Now, we have all made our decisions, yes?' he says.

We all nod in unison.

'Avon, Cliff, who is your vote for?'

Avon and I share a nod of confirmation. 'Viola.' he says.

She takes the news as expected, giving us a sarcastic smile, full of scorn and contempt.

'And Alex, Viola, who is your vote for?' Viola doesn't wait to fire her shot back.

'Avon.' she says, raising her eyebrows gleefully.

'Okay,' Doc says, 'the two of you, wait here, Alex, Cliff, follow me.'

He exits the room and leads us into the main entrance hall, out of earshot of the unit. We gather. 'When you have made your decision, meet us back inside.' he says, returning to the medical room.

Hendon stands at the entrance, looking strangely ambivalent. We turn to face each other. 'We're in the final three.' Alex says with a happy surprise.

'I know.' I return, with equal surprise. She moves closer and lowers her voice.

'Technically, we can control the game at this point. I asked Doc earlier about the prize again. He said we can have whatever we want, money's no object. However, there's no prize when there's only two of us left, we'd obviously vote for each other. The last point that you can win a prize is the final three. I think we can both agree that we have been suspicious of Avon from the get-go. So, the only question is, do we vote out Avon now, possibly including Viola in the prize pool, or do we vote out Viola now, which would be funnier, thus ensuring that she wouldn't be involved in any prize.'

'But what if she's the robot?' I say.

'Well I wouldn't have any qualms about involving Avon in a prize if we're right but if we're being honest, surely she isn't.'

'So why would we vote for her?' I say, not meaning to protect her, it's more of a tactical inquiry. 'Because she's not a very nice person. I've heard her and other people talk about her life and her difficulties and it's awful, it really is. I don't know if she thinks it allows her to be rude and obnoxious and use people and treat people like shit but I'm not having it. Some people have terrible things happen to them and they still treat people with respect and dignity. She's just a nasty person and I would derive pleasure from seeing her exiting a game that she has made very clear to everyone that she would like to win.'

Alex is clearly upset with Viola and sees this is an ideal opportunity to get her. I can't really argue, I've found Viola to be quite abrasive and easily the most difficult person here this evening. I'm fairly certain she isn't the robot though, so again, it would be a wasted chance. 'Okay. Let's vote her out.' I say.

Alex nods her head, smiles and leads me back into the medical unit. Doc, Avon and Viola stand together, deep in discussion. When they see us, they stop and spread out around us, forming an intimate circle.

'Have you made your decision?' Doc says, charging the atmosphere. 'Yes.' Alex says.

'Who is your robot?' he says.

'Cliff?' she says gently, looking at me to reveal our decision. Thanks Alex. 'Viola.' I say weakly, readying myself for a tirade of abuse.

Avon looks relieved. Viola is ready to blow.

'I don't know why you voted for me; I'm not leaving. Think again.' she says defiantly. Doc steps in.

'Come now, you have been selected, let's go to the gurney and introduce your arm to the needle.'

'No chance.' she says.

'Look, there's no need for this. I don't want to get Hendon involved and have an ugly scene unfold.'

'Get him involved, I'll knock him out!' she exclaims.

Doc backs away from her and gives the rest of us a look to do the same.

'Hendon? Can you escort our guest to the gurney please?' he calls to the huge frame at the threshold. Hendon approaches Viola, wearing a blank expression.

'Don't even think about it,' Viola says, waving her fists, 'you don't know who you're messing with.'

Viola moves into a fighting stance; I wouldn't have had her down as a brawler but she has a look in her eye. Knowing her as I do, I expect it's over-confidence.

When Hendon closes in on her, she throws two straight jabs with her left. Neither make contact but she has used them to disguise a right hook, which is flying towards his face.

Hendon hasn't raised his arms into a fighting pose until this point, quickly bringing up his left forearm to block the shot, whilst simultaneously throwing a straight right which lands flush on her jaw. Her eyes roll back and her body goes limp, but Hendon is moving like a dancer, using his arms to catch her and hold her body into his chest securely in one swift move. He sweeps her onto the gurney gracefully and swivels back to the entrance. Alex, Avon and I are

open-mouthed, almost impressed with his devastating efficiency. 'Thanks.' Doc says, seemingly unimpressed.

He walks to the unconscious body on the table and begins to go through the motions. The rest of us are still trying to compute the previous ten seconds. Hendon still has his calm, almost disinterested demeanour.

'That was a bit drastic.' Doc says.

Hendon grunts. Doc waits for the print out.

'I feel I must apologise to our guests on your behalf.' he says, addressing the three of us. 'Hendon is a sensitive soul but has a very black or white conscience. He doesn't make a habit of hitting people but I'm sure he felt that the situation needed that kind of response. You may think that I'm cruel to him but he responds to a direct approach and he knows that I trust him implicitly. The two of us will often play chess into the night, I'm no slouch but I can count on one hand the amount of victories I've attained. He tends the gardens and houseplants with care and attention, he's a delicate monster and my best friend.'

Hendon looks out of the room, clearly uncomfortable with

hearing praise. The three of us are too shocked to retort. It was drastic, I don't really know what to think.

'Human.' Doc announces, showing the incomprehensible printout to the room.

'Hendon, can you take Viola to her car. If she wakes, make sure to apologise and if she's angry, don't do it again.'

'She won't wake.' Hendon states, throwing her lifeless body over his shoulder like a rag doll and marching out of the front door.

Doc turns to us and thinks carefully before speaking.

'Here we are then, the final three, your last chance to win whatever your heart desires. Even I am surprised that our artifice has outwitted you and remains an obstacle to victory. Two of you are indeed humans. One of you is our creation, our vision. I'm incredibly proud.'

Hendon returns, stopping Doc in his tracks.

'I was trying to deliver a speech to our guests, full of whimsy and joy and you've come back in, banging the door and huffing and puffing. I forgot what I was saying now, thanks for that Hendon.' he says, full of sarcasm.

Hendon doesn't know how to respond.

'Go to the downstairs drawing room and fix drinks. Do after dinner liqueurs, coffee, whisky, that sort of thing. We'll be down in a moment.'

Hendon grunts, crossing the room and exiting. Doc is struggling to remember what he was on about and aborts.

'The time is nigh. The game is simple. I will speak to each of you for a few minutes, in private, leaving the other two to discuss what they will. After which, you will vote for your machine. Not the most annoying or obnoxious. I think this evening has taught you that choosing the difficult customer has brought no rewards. Follow me!'

Doc quickly exits, presumably heading to the downstairs drawing room. A lot of houses I have been in don't even have a drawing room, let alone more than one, which Doc insinuates.

We follow Doc across the hall and down another corridor, full of doors and art and decadence. I think if I guess correctly and win whatever my heart desires, I may choose to live here. It's not necessarily my style but I'm intrigued by the vastness, you could spend days exploring rooms and areas that you've never seen before.

The walk is brisk enough to keep the three of us from engaging, but Doc stands by an open door, ushering us inside.

I've no desire to describe the room, it's fantastic. Hendon stands by a small but well stocked bar, making various drinks and lining them up.

'Please, help yourself to a drink, I won't be a moment.' Doc says, retreating through a door at the back of the room and closing it behind him.

Avon takes what looks like a whisky, Alex and I choose a similar liquid in a similar glass. We all quaff and look around the room.

Light pours in through a two-way window from the back of the room. It reveals what is best described as a police interrogation room. Basic and without dressing, a table with a folding chair on either side. Stark and vapid. Doc is in there, straightening the chairs and wiping the table.

The room is nothing like what we have seen before. He returns to the doorway and speaks. 'The trickiest parts regarding the prosthetics were, ironically, the things that aren't on display. Inner ears and mouths, the tonsils took forever…the genitalia, the toenails. Obviously, the fingernails came first but having to emulate the procedure ten times, knowing that there was an excellent chance that they would never come under scrutiny. Then there was the eating and drinking problem. After many extravagant and complicated attempts, a small, sealed receptacle, just past the throat was the answer. The contents are collected and disposed of; we program the robot to entertain a certain amount without putting stress on the container. I think if Desmond was the robot, we would have had a malfunction, he was putting it away! We argued for hours about giving the machine the ability to produce saliva. I was personally against the idea, thinking it was superfluous. Thankfully, I was in the minority because it was one of the first things you

used to distinguish the culprit. Still, it is what it is and here we are. I will invite you into this room alphabetically for a brief chat. After which, we will head to the medical unit for a final round of voting. Alex?'

He beckons her and she accepts, finishing her drink and placing it on the desk. He closes the door and Avon and I watch as they sit on either side of the table. Avon picks up her discarded glass and inhales.

'What are you doing?' I ask. 'Just checking.' he replies. 'For what?'

'I'm making sure it has an alcoholic smell.' 'And?'

'It seems legit…'

'Have you started to turn your attention away from me Avon? It's a bit late in the day.' I say, half-joking.

He turns to me with a serious expression etched on his face. 'What do you think of her?'

'Who, Alex?' I say.

'Yeah. I mean, she's been flying under the radar all evening. Avoiding suspicion, keeping a clever distance. It's the kind of behaviour a machine would incorporate, no? She's stayed neutral and reserved her opinions. The only other person who has displayed similar tendencies is you.'

'And you've had it in for me all night!' I say, again, half-joking. 'That may be so but seriously Cliff, what do you think?'

I study Alex through the glass, watching her and Doc exchanging communication. 'I don't think so, Avon...'

'Look, I think if I was responsible for building a robot, there would be certain parameters to follow. As I've said before, I think my image is too old, if you don't mind me saying, I think you're too short. Alex seems to be an ideal age, height, weight. She is aesthetically pleasing.'

I understand what he's saying. Out of the three of us, she is the most pleasing on the eye, with a classic, almost generic profile. Visually, it would make sense. I nod along in agreement.

'Cliff, I'll be straight with you. I think it's you. It's only watching her over this last minute or so, I've begun to wonder if it's Alex that's been hiding in plain sight all along. I'm gonna vote for you unless we can agree on this. Consider it. It has to be a possibility?'

'It is a possibility Avon. The problem I have is that I have had no inclination to vote for her and out of the three of us, from things that have transpired this evening, my guess would be you.' Avon does his best Hendon grimace.

'Well this is the most likely scenario then. We will vote for each other and she will get the swing vote and a place in the last two. When she comes out of there and I go in, you will have a chance to persuade her to vote for me. Then you will go in and I will do everything in my power to get her to vote for you.'

'In fairness, this game has been going on for a while with people trying to cajole each other into collusion. Nearly everyone has asked me to vote with them, including you, we're not really voting purely, it's probably why we've been getting it wrong all night. You think it's me but all of a sudden, you entertain the idea of teaming up to get Alex out.'

'No, it's not that. I'm trying to be open-minded and consider the possibility…a possibility that exists.'

Silence falls, taking the spark from an escalating debate. Both of us look at her, wondering. She and Doc stand, still conversing but seemingly reaching their conclusion. It feels as if Avon and I have done the same. Doc releases Alex back to the room and gestures to Avon. Avon looks at me with an expression that is difficult to describe. Stern but accepting? He and Doc shut the door behind them, leaving Alex and I alone.

'What happened in there?' I say.

'He asked me not to discuss it. What happened out here?'
'Avon and I talked about the possibility of it being you.' Alex smiles.

'And how did you reach that opinion?'

'Well, frankly, we thought that you were aesthetically the likely candidate. Height, weight, appearance, that sort of thing.'

She smiles again.

'Maybe they needed to house the electronics tightly and chose a more compact structure, like you. Or maybe there's loads of internal equipment that needs to be housed in a larger structure, like Avon. The question doesn't really hold a lot of weight. Unless you could see the internal equipment required, you're guessing as to how much room you'd need. I have a question for you that might be more productive though.'

I'm listening.

'Doc seems satisfied that the machine is blending in, how perfect do you think it is? Has its personality got flaws and physical traits, like all humans do? If so, I think Avon has been slightly more…outspoken? Not the right word. Unorthodox? Alternative? You know what I'm saying?'

'I think so, but it must be incredibly difficult to install those things in a machine.'

'In which case, the likelihood is you. You've carefully straddled the line all evening.' 'So have you.' I say.

Alex is looking through the glass.

'If they have made a machine so wonderful, I think it would have those flaws, it would be apparent if it didn't. I think it might be him.'

We both watch Avon, the way he moves and talks. The way he reacts to conversation. It's smooth, flawless. I'm still thinking about what Alex discussed with Doc. Curiosity killed the cat but I try again.

'So can you tell me anything about what was said in there?' She turns her attention to me.

'He asked me not to say anything. There's nothing to worry about though, it was sort of a memory test. He asked questions relating to me and my past mainly. Stop thinking about it, it's just a casual exchange. That's all I'm going to say.'

That didn't satisfy me, I'll still worry until I'm in there but

Alex isn't forward with the details so I change tact.

'So, who will you vote for?'

'I'm not sure, the decision is swinging back and forth, you?'

I decide to tell the truth, although the truth can change between now and then. 'Him.' I say.

Alex slowly shakes her head. 'Why.'

'I've just got a feeling.'

'Would that feeling have something to do with the fact that he's voted for you a bit this evening?' she says playfully.

I smile.

'It would, I think he talked you up but when it comes to the crunch, he'll vote for me.' 'We'll see…'

Avon looks emotional in there, sad and welling up somewhat. He takes a tissue from Doc and uses it to disguise his reaction.

'You see this?' I ask. 'Yeah.' she replies.

'What?' I say, noting the questionable way in which she responded.

'I'm just saying, would a machine be able to cry? Would it be able to produce tears?' 'Probably not. He's not actually crying though…'

'Yeah but you saw, he was glassy eyed.'

'Yeah,' I ponder, 'it's odd. What can they be talking about in there?' 'Maybe something difficult from his past.' Alex says, turning to me.

I turn to her and we look at each other's faces closely. Studying for telltale signs. I think she has realised as I have, that perhaps Avon isn't the robot because of the apparent emotion. She looks real though. The problem is that we all do.

'The robot can eat and drink so it stands to reason that they integrated an ability to cry, surely? Perhaps Doc is testing out the muscle?'

'Perhaps…' I say, sounding uncertain.

Avon and Doc stand and make their way to the exit. Alex and I share a worried look. 'Cliff?' Doc beckons me in.

Avon walks over to us. I pass him and enter the back room. Immediately I become aware of the temperature drop.

'Hendon, go and get the equipment from the medical unit please.' Doc says, before closing the door behind him.

'Take a seat Cliff.'

We both sit, either side of the desk. I look through the glass at the other two who are already conversing and glancing back at me. I wonder what they're talking about.

'Now then, Cliff, I have four questions for you. There's nothing to worry about, I asked Alex and Avon the same four questions and question one is more of a rhetorical question really. I already know the answer and it is meant to cast a seed of doubt into your mind. The first question is "What is your favourite colour?" After you think for a moment, the answer you will give is "Purple." When you were very young, pre-teen, the answer would be green. The purpose of this is to make you wonder how I could possibly know that. Maybe we've researched all of our investors thoroughly so we could make this evening's entertainment as realistic as possible. Or maybe you are in fact a machine that we have programmed with these tastes, therefore knowing precisely what your preferences are. I can see bewilderment in your eyes and that's exactly what question one is primed for. Now question two. At any point tonight, have you considered the idea that you might be the machine?'

I'm reeling. How could he know that? Purple is my favourite colour but I don't wear purple clothing or collect purple things, it's just something I think really. I don't make it obvious or known particularly. I can't fathom how he would know that.

'I haven't until now.' I say. Doc smiles.

'It's okay, the other two could only manage a similar response when I made a revelation that blew their minds. I can see you're visibly shaken so I'll move on. Question three. If you guess the machine correctly, what will your prize selection be?'

I think for a moment, trying to gather my shit. Paranoia reigns as I look through the glass to see the other two, watching me and talking to each other, plotting my downfall.

'I would live here.' I say. Doc smiles again.

'It's ironic Cliff! Alex and Avon said the same thing! If two of you get this right, you'll have to squabble over bedrooms! That said, the sprawling grounds would probably mean you wouldn't see much of each other anyway. The irony of course, is that one of you already lives here. The machine has yet to venture from the complex. Still, your wish is granted.'

He looks content and begins to stand. 'Is there a fourth question?' I ask.

'There is, who is your robot?' he says nonchalantly. 'Are we doing this now?'

'We are. The other two have already cast their votes, we just need yours and I will reveal the decision out there.'

I'm a little off-guard.

'What if we all vote for each other? You know, we get one vote each?'

'If that happens, the three of you will have an uncomfortable, face-to-face discussion until a decision is made. If a decision can't be reached, then I'm afraid you will get in your cars and travel home, none the wiser. Hopefully, that anticlimax can be avoided though, we'll see. Have you made a decision?'

I look at the two of them on the other side of the glass, watching with anticipation. I cover my mouth with my hand, foolishly concerned about lipreading and speaking quietly, in case there's a microphone or something.

'Avon.' I say. Doc nods.

'Follow me.' he says, rising from his seat and hastily entering the main room.

The three of us stand around Doc, waiting for the outcome. Hendon has returned with the equipment and hovers nearby, poised for action.

'Well, you have all cast your vote and I'm delighted to tell you that there's no need for further action, a decision has been reached. I will reveal the result in the reverse order in which you came into me, which will heighten the drama as Cliff has just voted for Avon and before that, Avon voted for Cliff.'

Avon and I smile at each other, an accepting smile. Doc continues.

'Alex pondered over her decision for a while, given the circumstances, she's probably mortified by the importance but there it is. She voted for Avon. Will you roll up your sleeve please?'

Doc walks to Hendon and takes the needle and machinery. Avon stalls.

'Look, I don't really like needles. I did the test earlier so you already know the outcome. I mean, you know who the robot is anyway, is there really any need?'

Doc grins, readying the gear.

'You're right Avon. I could tell the room that you aren't the machine. That there is no reward to offer as it has successfully tricked all of you. That you, Avon, are in fact, the owner of the worst position tonight. You have lasted all evening but still leave without knowing the truth. However, I'm afraid it wouldn't be sufficient. None of you would be completely satisfied with this resolution. There would be a sliver of doubt. Humans believe what they see, not necessarily what they're told. Seeing is more tangible, undeniable.'

Hendon has slowly wandered behind Avon, gently moving closer. 'I understand Doc, I just hate needles and think it's superfluous.' 'I understand Avon but needs must.'

'I won't.'

Doc looks a little disappointed and raises his eyebrows to Hendon. Avon stands oblivious as Hendon wraps his arms around Avons neck and applies a sleeper hold. Thick biceps clench the air supply and Avon loses his posture after several seconds. Hendon slumps the unconscious body into a chair. Doc swiftly moves in with the needle.

'Thanks.' he manages.

Alex and I glance at each other, clearly feeling the tension. I'm glad she didn't vote for me. I'm especially glad I'm not the one in that chair. Maybe Avon is the machine. Maybe the game will be over in a moment and we can all be relieved and fight over prizes with laughter and a fondness for the evening's entertainment. Unfortunately though, Doc holds the machine up and grimaces.

'Human again.' he declares. 'So, there's no reward?' I say.

'Certainly not Cliff, there's no reward now. The guessing game is over. There's no sport anymore. You think it's Alex and Alex thinks it's you. All that remains is the big reveal. Hendon, would you carry our guest to his car and see that he's okay if he wakes up please?'

'He won't.' Hendon says, throwing another limp body over his shoulder skilfully and exiting the room.

Doc opens the door to the back room and gestures us in.

'Alex, Cliff, take a seat, I have a phone call to make before I join you, where I will give you final instructions. How exciting!'

Alex and I enter the room and sit opposite each other. Doc closes us in and we see him making a phone call in the main room.

'Here we are then,' Alex says, 'it's me or you.'

Chapter Nine
The End of The End of The End.

She doesn't seem very excited to be here, understandable really. 'Are you alright?' I ask.

'Not really,' she says, 'I feel terrible.'

'Why?'

Alex sighs, struggling to meet my eyes.

'When you were in there with Doc, I asked Avon what they had talked about when he was in there and that you and I had thought that he looked upset. Basically, he told me that Doc had become quite a close friend over the last year. Avon was a hedge fund director and his company made enormous amounts of money by predicting which companies would succeed and fail during the global pandemic. During lockdown, his company made a killing. What they were doing wasn't illegal, but it was certainly immoral. Avon struggled with the morality and so began his descent into anxiety, insomnia, and depression. Then his wife contracted the virus and died. Avon said he quit the business immediately and stayed at home for a year, living like a hermit, addicting himself to painkillers and crying constantly. Then he met Doc last year, donated his fortune to this enterprise and slowly began to feel better, without the financial weight around his neck. Apparently, they attend various social events together and help each other with day-to-day struggles.'

'Crikey, that's heavy.' I say.

'I know. He was becoming emotional talking about it. It was so real, at that moment, I just knew he wasn't a robot.'

'But you'd already voted for him.' Alex nods solemnly.

'I told him. When Doc was revealing the result, he already knew the outcome. I feel terrible about it.'

'Look,' I say, 'it's all part of the game, it's just a game, don't worry Alex.' I'm trying to offer her comfort but I can see it's changing nothing.

The door opens and Doc walks in, shifting the dynamic. 'Then there were two!' he exclaims proudly.

Seeing that neither of us are sharing his enthusiasm, he changes gears.

'I have updated our scientists and they have started the process of shutting down our machine. The guilty party will be left with twenty percent power, the innocent human will begin to notice the reduction in the other, making for a suitable finale. This procedure will take several minutes to execute, giving you enough time to talk about your pasts or share war stories. Maybe you should talk about your scars?' he says cryptically.

'Whatever you decide to do, thank you for coming this evening and taking part in the festivities. Thank you for supporting the Krelboyne Institute and I will see you shortly.'

Doc closes his eyes and bows. He's a strange one. He opens and shuts the door behind him, leaving us with a parting shot.

'I was talking to the human, of course.'

Alex and I are left alone, contemplating the situation. I look through the glass window, into the main room. Doc has sat at a desk, Hendon, usually on the periphery, has pulled up a chair and sits next to him. They converse but Doc doesn't take his eyes from us, watching like a hawk. I turn back to Alex, who appears to be undoing her trousers and sliding them down. I'm unsure of what I'm looking at and glance away respectfully.

'What are you doing?' I ask. 'Look.' she says.

I do, she's drawing my attention to a large, faded scar on her right thigh.

She begins to dress.

'I fell off of my horse when I was sixteen. His hoof stood on my leg, popping it like a balloon. I had three operations and I was in a wheelchair for eleven months. They said I may never walk again. I disguise a limp as best I can and still take medication for the pain. I can feel it now, aching. I'm not a robot.'

She's finished with her belt and stares at me with insistence.

I roll up my left shirt sleeve, revealing a smaller scar that runs up the inside of my forearm.

'I wrapped my arm the wrong way around a goalpost when I was thirteen. I had an operation, plates and pins, it never healed properly. It's not as drastic as yours but it's there alright.' Alex leans across the table for a closer examination.

'One of us has been programmed with the memory. A scar might indicate an area that has particular wiring inside or maybe it's just to add realism. I'm not sure what it means…'

She sits back in her chair, dissatisfied.

'This has become a nightmare,' she says, 'at the start of the game, it seemed fun and quite exciting but now, I'm just starting to panic. What if it's me? Everything I think I know has been planted there, purposefully. Are you worried?'

'I am, yes, although I feel certain of my memories, my past, I remember things throughout my life, feelings.'

'But so do I! One of us has obviously had them installed!' Alex emphasises. She's becoming anxious, fidgeting in her seat and her breathing has quickened.

'Earlier, Doc said that the machine has never left the complex. I remember the car journey here, giving my keys and phone to the driver, he put them in the glove compartment. I remember it, do you remember your drive here?'

'Not vividly but yes, I do remember the drive here.' I say. Alex rubs her forehead desperately.

'So one of us has had that programmed, a memory that isn't real? Like everything else, our entire life is a fabrication. Do you remember your entire life?'

'It's patchy but yeah, I can remember it all.' I say. 'Go on then, tell me.'

I shift in my seat for a better purchase.

'Okay. Jacques Moreau was born in 1902. His mother died during childbirth, his father was a dentist. His early years were bereft of nurture. His father struggled with the death of his wife and as an only child himself, had no family to fill in the gaps. When Jacques was twelve, his father was called up to fight in the war and left Jacques to fend for himself. Despite the lack of education, Jacques became skilled at woodwork and maths, understanding measurements and using his own initiative. At fifteen, he joined the war, I think the legal age was nineteen but they needed the bodies and it's well documented that it wasn't strictly enforced. Fighting for his country seemed like the right thing to do but the main reason was obviously so that he could find his father, he missed his father. In 1918, he returned to an empty home, his father was killed on duty. He was sixteen, uneducated, alone.'

Alex appears to be calmer and seems interested in where this story leads, so I continue.

'He got a job in a small vegetable store, living in the bedsit above. In his spare time he would continue making strange wooden toys with moving parts. These toys were rudimentary and rather crude but he was more concerned with how they worked than how they looked. Over

time, the quality of his work increased, he began to make a name for himself locally, selling the odd item and starting to earn more from his art than his job. People started to regard him as something of a genius, with his moving parts becoming more sophisticated and complex. He was invited to a chateau on the outskirts of Biarritz, to show his work to the wealthy elitists. They bought everything he had for large lumps of cash. It was there that he met Amelia, the daughter and heiress to the chateau in which they were standing. She adored his origins, he was unlike any of the people she would usually rub shoulders with. It was love. She moved him in immediately and they were inseparable. It was 1934. In 1936, her parents were killed when their boat sank in the Pacific. She inherited the chateau and in 1938 they had their son, Henri. The next year, Amelia was due to give birth to twins but they all died during the labour. Jacques was devastated. She had named him in her will as the inheritor of her wealth and suddenly, he and Henri would share the chateau with eighty plus staff during the war and into the nineteen fifties. In 1954, unable to hold onto the grief and sinking in isolation, Jacques hung himself in the barn. Henri found his father, he was sixteen years old.'

The room is plunged into darkness. After a few seconds of

silence, the light returns as instantly as it went. Maybe a brief power cut? I look through the glass, Doc and Hendon stare back, unmoved. Alex is wearing a smirk.

'It's a nice story Cliff, it feels…scripted? The way you're delivering it feels unnatural, I dunno.' 'That seems harsh, I'm recounting my life in detail in an attempt to show you that it is you, and not me.'

Alex scratches her eyebrow, unconvinced.

'Go on then, I'm listening, what happened to the boy?'

'Over the following decade, Henri slowly adjusted to a life of luxury and loneliness. Wracked with grief and unjustified guilt, why did his father do that? Maybe if he was a better son? He didn't understand and blamed himself. So, naturally I suppose, he followed in his fathers footsteps and began to master the woodwork and moving parts. It made him feel closer to his father somehow. He incorporated metalwork and hydraulics into his designs, surpassing Jacques' complexities and gaining his own style. Nearly always creating something with human characteristics, obsessing with joints, elbows, knees, wrists. Once he felt his creations were adequate, he began making arms and legs with fully moving joints. The staff at the chateau urged him to show his labour in a public setting and in 1967, he took his work on a local tour, wowing the audiences with his projects. Inundated with requests to purchase his work, he refused, he didn't need the money and the pieces had become his closest allies over the years. He felt bonded to them and felt they were a link to Jacques.

A week after he returned to the safety of the chateau, a visitor came to the door, requesting a sit down with Henri. Her name was Nancy Jones, she was the owner of a large estate in Bath, England. She was in a similar situation to him, scuttling around a large, empty home. Her husband had died and left her in possession of seventy acres of land and she and her teenage daughter, Barbara, would rarely see each other. Their relationship had broken down after he passed and the untimely death of Barbara's twin brother, Richard, six months after. She insisted that Henri should take his work to the next level, building a head with moving features, a neck that swivelled realistically and a torso made from clay, formed accurately and supporting the other parts. He could actually form his ideas into a complete picture. Nancy said that he'd created wonderful pieces of a puzzle and wanted to see the finished product.

They liked each other and, inspired, Henri set to work on his next project.

In 1970, after exchanging several letters to each other from across the sea, Nancy and her daughter visited Henri for the summer. Henri's project had faltered and though the three of them were affable, Nancy was disappointed with the progress he had made, occasionally remarking on the evidence. This drove a wedge between them, which was the perfect scenario for the daughter.

Barbara was nineteen and disliked her mother. She had begun drinking alcohol and experimenting with drugs, comfortable in her opulent surroundings with no talent and no desire to make her own way. The only black mark in her life was Nancy.

When she saw Henri's lifestyle she began to formulate a plan. Henri was thirty-two, dishevelled and unaccustomed to human contact. Barbara was attractive and trim. She began paying him attention, laughing at his jokes and stroking his arms, commenting on how hairy they were and telling him that she loved the sensation on her skin, paving the way for more physical connection. It was bordering on the obscene. Nancy was appalled at how they were carrying on and told them so. Her and Nancy had a blazing row and had to be pulled apart by several of the staff. Henri, completely out of his element, took a back seat and watched the fire burn. At the end of summer, Nancy returned to England, alone. Barbara stayed with Henri, sinking her teeth deeper into her victim.

The first year together, as it normally is in relationships, was the happiest. Henri let his work slide but didn't care, he'd never felt special or loved before and couldn't believe his luck. He was in dreamland. He had no idea that Barbara was feigning these feelings and slowly convincing him to hand over his life, willingly.

Barbara decided that the best way to tighten the noose would be pregnancy, but after several months of enduring the ritual, it was clear that one of them, if not both, were failing this task. She started to let the mask slip, frustration led to arguments and the drinking moved up a gear. Henri wasn't well versed in dealing with human emotion and consistently fell short of her demands. He took full responsibility for being unable to conceive and she would belittle him furiously, every time she had a drink in her hand, which was every time she was awake. It was untenable.

Neither of them working or even engaging in hobbies or activities. They were both rattling around the chateau, her drunk and him confused. The staff became disillusioned and began to dwindle, finding opportunity elsewhere. The rooms became unkempt, the gardens overgrown. The property had lost its sparkle. It was a toxic atmosphere that was draining everything.

Then, in 1974, a chance encounter that had the potential to change everything.'

Alex was listening closely. She still wore a dubious expression but was leaning towards me, engrossed.

I glance through the glass and see that Alex, the other Alex, has joined Doc and Hendon. This is what it must be like to live in a fish tank. Suddenly, I have a thought. We met the other Alex earlier, she was lead scientist or something, what if she gave the machine her own name in a weird, egotistical, self-homage? I mean, some people give their children their own name, the common man has taken a few examples of upper-class formality in recent times. Double barrel surnames have become quite normal these days. I look back at the Alex in front of me.

They certainly don't look similar but still, has the answer been this simple all along? She grows tired of my seemingly pregnant pause and nudges me along.

'Well! A chance encounter?'

I notice that she's pronouncing her words slowly, almost slurring. Maybe she's winding down? I won't say anything, maybe it's my hearing.

'There was a knock at the door. Fortunately, Henri was in earshot because the usual servant had left for pastures new and there was no replacement and no arrangements for it either. He hadn't the first idea or the wherewithal to address such things. Upon opening, a woman, who lived in the nearest village was looking distressed and explained that she had to go to the police station and make a statement. She'd been burgled and her apartment had been ransacked. As the woman asked if it would be okay to leave her child there while she went, she actively pushed the boy across the threshold, taking any decision away from Henri. She thanked him and told him she'd be no more than an hour, retreating down the steps and into the passenger seat of a man's car. Henri stood motionless at the entrance and watched as the two embraced passionately and sped away.

He took the boy inside and they made sandwiches together. Sitting at the dining table and getting to know each other, there was an immediate alliance. Henri hadn't noticed the time fly and they talked for hours and played swingball in the garden. The boy was eight years old and had never experienced the attention or the fun before. The feeling was mutual, Henri was happy for the first time in a long time.

When it started to get dark, Henri realised that it had been over five hours since the boy had been left in his company. He had no number or any way of reaching the woman, he didn't even know her name. He asked the boy, but the boy told him that neither of them had a name, which Henri thought was strange.

He decided that the boy would spend the night, he had ample space and would make a room up. The two of them spent several minutes wandering the halls, looking for a member of staff to aid them but to no avail. Henri had no idea how to make a bed so went to Barbara's room to ask for assistance. She was drunk but coherent and as Henri explained the situation, her eyes lit up and she moved closer to the boy, eventually wrapping her arms around him, like a Python, coiling around its victim's neck.

Together, the three of them dressed the bed in the adjoining room and Barbara took a fresh bottle of Gin in with her, spending the night with the boy, stroking his hair and drinking heavily. She was happy to give her affection to someone other than Henri, which was fortuitous at the time, as the boy's mother never did come back.

It was six weeks before Christmas and those six weeks were the happiest that any of them had ever been.

Both Henri and Barbara revelled in giving their attention to someone else. Henri would show the boy his bizarre contraptions and began to teach him how to invent his own. Barbara would mollycoddle the boy, throwing endless love and money at any problem that arose. The boy had never known anything like it and couldn't comprehend the luxury.

Well then came January and February, cold and cruel. Snow that didn't lay but enough to make the outdoors treacherous. The arguments became louder and more vitriolic. Barbara's dissatisfaction was prevalent and idol threats that she made about returning to England began to carry more weight. Eventually, after a long phone conversation with her mother, the cavalry arrived and whisked her and the boy away to Bath.

Henri was distraught and begged her not to take the boy. He threw himself on the car that was sent for Barbara, demanding a different outcome. The boy was crying, it was a traumatic scene. Two men from the accompanying vehicle removed Henri from his human barrier stance and beat him to a bloody pulp, right there in front of them. It was harrowing. The boy never saw him again.

In Bath, Barbara continued on her alcoholic slide, her mother by this time, too self-important and aloof to get involved. The boy always felt her coldness and was often blamed for the decline of her daughter. Sometimes he believed her but knew in his heart that that train had left the station, long before he'd arrived. He wasn't a blood relative, and Nancy could never fully accept that, there was always an unspoken wall of resentment between them. He missed Henri and wished he'd stayed with him, a man that in later life, he'd refer to warmly, as his father. But that's life I suppose.'

Alex looks at me almost scornfully, swimming in doubt.

'So you're telling me your life story, so I'm assuming that the boy you keep referring to is you. I'm sitting here doing the maths and it doesn't work. He arrived at the chateau in 1974, when he was eight. That means the boy was born in 1966, give or take. That means that today, the boy would be around sixty. You're never sixty Cliff. You could get away with forty but never sixty.' 'Maybe the boy is my father?' I say defiantly.

'Then why would you keep calling him the boy? I don't understand the mentality behind it. In fact, thinking about it now, the only person here who could fit that story is Doc. He told us earlier that he studied in Bristol, which isn't a million miles from Bath. It almost makes sense. Maybe you've been programmed with his backstory, complete with emotion and accuracy. I'm calling it. I think it's you Cliff.'

As Alex says my name, she stops dead. As if someone has pressed pause. Frozen in time. Halfway through gesturing and halfway through smiling a smile of recognition. I don't believe it. It's her. Powered down and stuck in time. Adrenaline and relief rush around my body. I've done it, I've won. Well, I haven't won anything, but I've sort of won the game. I must admit, I was getting worried there. Was everything I knew and everything I feel, a fabrication? I glance through the glass to accept my acclaim from the audience, the three of them are looking back, happy and smiling. I go to walk over to Alex for a closer inspection, but my legs aren't responding to what my brain is asking of them. I attempt to use my arms to push up off the table but again, nothing happens.

Confused, I glance through the glass again, aware that my neck isn't turning, only my eyes. Doc, Hendon and other Alex are looking back, happy and smiling. Only this time, I realise that they aren't moving either. Like Alex, they are frozen. I don't know what's happening.

Then, like a click of the fingers, they vanish, as if someone turned off a light. Opposite me, Alex has vanished too. I sit alone in the room, completely mystified.

Then it starts to dawn on me and I have that sinking feeling. It's me. There must be a delay in visual cognition or something because what I'm experiencing isn't normal. It's devastating. I'm devastated.

There's another flash of darkness and then I'm back in the main part of the room, sitting in a wheelchair. Hendon is escorting Alex out of the door, she looks back at me with wonder and adoration but I'm unable to respond. It's like my brain is working perfectly but I am unable to share my thoughts and feelings. My body is a cage.

Doc and other Alex stand before me, proudly cooing over their achievement. 'Can he hear us?' she says.

'He can. He's on full shutdown now but there'll be a few minutes of awareness.' Doc replies. 'How dreadful.' she says.

Every few seconds I blackout briefly. I miss slivers of the conversation they are having but they continue to stare at me, fascinated.

'Will he remember anything of tonight?' she says.

'He won't. We'll do further tests on him over the coming days and continue the improvements.' 'He did well tonight, he can't be that far from the finished article.'

Doc turns to her sternly.

'There is always room for improvement.' he states.

She nods. The blackouts start to last for an increasing amount of time. Large segments evade me. Memories fade. I struggle to recount my name. Cliff or Clive or... Doc is saying something, feeling my face but, I hear nothing, I feel nothing.

Hendon stands over me, separating my torso from my legs, Doc helps. 'Careful Hendon, this is one of my best suits, gently!'

I watch him carefully place my legs onto the floor and turning back, he reaches inside of my stomach, removing a transparent box containing liquid and half eaten pizza bits. Doc sets about removing my head from my neck, placing me on a desk. They converse but my hearing has stopped so I can only see their lips move.

The blackouts are taking over. They have put my head into a box. There is light above me but not around me. I am at peace. The lid is on and I am consumed by darkness. I close my eyes.

Printed in Great Britain
by Amazon